Presented To:

_____

From:

_____

Date:

_____

Elves of Zeoch

THE LAST TWO

Elves of Zeoch

THE LAST TWO

Kaden Hurley

Illustrations by Phil George.

philgeorgeillustration@yahoo.com

Ambient:

An imprint of Destiny Image

This book and all other Destiny Image, Revival Press, MercyPlace, Fresh Bread, Destiny Image Fiction, and Treasure House books are available at Christian bookstores and distributors worldwide.

For a U.S. bookstore nearest you, call 1-800-722-6774.

For more information on foreign distributors, call 717-532-3040.

Reach us on the Internet: www.destinyimage.com.

ISBN 13 TP: 978-0-7684-3936-6
ISBN 13 Ebook: 978-0-7684-8945-3

For Worldwide Distribution, Printed in the U.S.A.

1 2 3 4 5 6 7 8 9 10 11 / 13 12 11

Dedication

This book is dedicated to my fourth grade teacher, Miss Jennifer Heishman.

I have wanted to write a book for years. Thank you for giving me the confidence to start and finish one.

Acknowledgments

I would like to thank my mom, Kelly Hurley, and my gram, Norma Keefer, for encouraging me and for being my first editors. My dad, Shea Hurley, and sister, Jenna Hurley, also deserve a huge thank you for being my inspiration for Barron and Ebeny. I would also like to thank my best friends, Rebekah Dehart and Zachary Gantz, for being my support from the beginning to the end.

Contents

The Secret Valley of the Elves
Saya Mountains
Kakeet River
Galvis
Pluma
Galee Forest
Terios
Zingle
Nahkohb
Jestae River
Froghorn's Territory
Won-Fa Dunes
Otahko Beach
Forbidden Mountains
Gorgon's Castle

Chapter 1

Unexpected Visitors

"Ha! That's the card I needed. I win!" Ebeny triumphantly shouted. Her light blue eyes sparkled with delight.

"Ugh, I could've used that one, too!" Camilla, Ebeny's older sister, groaned. "You won the last three games. I can't believe it," she added with a slight smile.

"Well, good job, Ebeny. I didn't see that coming," Uncle James praised warmly.

Ebeny smiled. "Thanks, Uncle James. Do you want to play another game?" she asked.

"Yeah," Camilla agreed intently.

"Of course. Here, I'll deal the cards," Uncle James offered.

Then, suddenly, the light above their heads flickered and went out. Uncle James sighed, collected the cards, and set them in a neat stack beside him. Rising from his seat, he said, "You two wait here. I'm going to check the rest of the house to see if the power is out everywhere or if it's just the light in this room."

When Uncle James returned, Ebeny and Camilla were standing by the window, watching the storm outside. He walked over behind them and rested a hand on each of their shoulders. All three of them gazed out the window at the pouring rain. "Well, the lights are out in the rest of the house, too. It's too dark to play another game of cards, but I think you should have enough light to finish cleaning your room," Uncle James said to the sisters.

"Wow. Cleaning our room. My favorite Saturday activity," Ebeny noted sarcastically. Camilla grinned at her sister, and they both trudged to the stairs to begin climbing.

On their way, Ebeny stopped to look at an old picture of her mother, Ariona. She was beautiful. Her red hair was lightly streaked with blond and tumbled in soft curls past her shoulders. Camilla and Ebeny always marveled at the color of their mother's hair and wondered why they hadn't inherited that striking color; Camilla's hair was a soft chestnut brown, and Ebeny's was as black as the midnight sky. Ariona's dazzling eyes were as blue as a clear summer sky. The sisters had no memories of their mother. Uncle James told them that both their parents had left them when Ebeny and Camilla were very young, but he would never say why or where they had gone. At least they had a photo of their mother; they had nothing with which to envision their father.

"OH MY GOSH! *What was that?!*" cried Camilla from the upstairs bedroom. Ebeny rushed up and got there just before Uncle James.

"Are you girls all right? Why did you shout?" He looked around the room, searching for the source of their distress.

"Uncle James! Over there by the window! A big hairy black thing! It just leaped off the windowsill, so I didn't get a good look at it," Camilla said breathlessly to them, her dark green eyes clouded with astonishment and fear.

Uncle James rushed to the rain-splattered window and peered into the morning gloom. Out of a nearby tree lunged a shaggy black creature with long, pointed teeth and sharp claws. It hurtled its bear-like body into the window, which shattered with the impact. Uncle James was thrown to the floor, but the beast was too massive to fit through the broken window. It gnashed its teeth in frustration at Uncle James. Quickly covering his hand with a nearby blanket, Uncle James snatched up a large shard of glass and plunged it into the monster's golden eye. The beast's high-pitched shriek pierced the air.

Dropping backward, the big beast twisted in mid-air and landed on all fours like a cat. It jumped up and raced half blind into the forest surrounding the house. Uncle James was breathing hard and leaning against the wall. Ebeny and Camilla were huddled together, terrified, in a corner.

"Blackess," murmured Uncle James. He stared blankly at the window. "I'm sorry, girls. I should have told you sooner. Come with me. We need to talk. And don't worry; he won't come back, not for a while at least." He tore his hard gaze away from the window to lead them down the stairway, stopping at the portrait of Ariona to tell them, "If your mother were here, she would scold me for not telling you before now. I guess I was just afraid of what would happen when I did."

The two sisters followed closely behind him. They sat down on the blue couch in front of the TV. "So what was that thing at the window?" Camilla asked him in a trembling voice as she sat down between Ebeny and Uncle James.

He reached up and acted like he was going to pull his dark brown hair out. He struggled to keep his face calm, but his green eyes betrayed his worries. Then he sighed and started to explain. "All right. First off, I am not Uncle James. I am Barron."

"Stop," Ebeny said. "What are you talking about?" Beside her, Camilla was mute with shock.

"I am not your uncle," Barron said again.

Camilla suddenly found her voice. "You mean you've been lying to us for all these years? How could you? Why?"

Barron sighed. "I didn't want to, but I couldn't risk the spies finding out who we really were. It was hard avoiding them, but I managed. I wanted to tell you all about this when you were old enough to fully understand."

"Spies?" Ebeny inquired.

"Sent from Gorgon." Barron raised his hand as Ebeny opened her mouth to ask another question. "I know you have many questions, but I will explain as much as I can." The sisters nodded and shut their mouths.

"Everything has to do with where we are originally from. We are from Zeoch, a world very different from the one we live in now. Zeoch is held tightly in the grip of a sorcerer named Gorgon. At first his heart and mind were in the right place, and everyone loved and respected him. Then things began to change. He was no longer satisfied with love and respect; he wanted power, all of it. In his quest for power, he abused many privileges and betrayed even the closest of friendships; he did a lot of things that no sane man would do. Regardless of how heinous his acts were, hordes of followers flocked to his side. For some of them, the opportunity to do evil was too much to resist. For others, it was simply easier to join him than to oppose him. When he had gathered enough men and creatures, Gorgon challenged the king of that time period." The way that he said the word *king* made Camilla suspicious, but she thought it was better to not interrupt him now.

Barron continued, "The battle that followed was a gruesome one. The king led a huge army of men, elves, giants, faeries, and an assortment of other creatures against Gorgon's forces. The king's army fought valiantly, but in the end, evil triumphed over good.

"Both sides suffered heavy losses, but the greatest loss was that of an entire race. The noble race of elves was obliterated during the battle. A group of men and other creatures, who had fought for the king and survived, quickly fled in an attempt to escape Gorgon's wrath. The king survived as well, but even he was forced to flee to another world." Uncle James paused to let everything sink in a little before continuing. The expression on the girls' faces showed him that it was too much all at once.

"Wait a minute. What are you talking about? Faeries? Giants? Elves? Those creatures aren't real. They only exist in fantasy stories, unless *we're* in a fantasy story right now."

Barron asked matter-of-factly, "Well now, Ebeny, did that creature at the window seem like a fantasy to you?" A sudden look of realization swept over her face.

"Good point. That big, hairy thing was totally real," Camilla breathed.

"Blackess, the thing that you saw on the window, is the first hand of Gorgon, like a personal assistant. And you don't want to cross his path. He has a howl that makes everything go cold. His claws are filled with a deadly type of poison that travels through the bloodstream incredibly fast and kills the victim in only a few minutes.

"Gorgon also has many gallops in his legion. Gallops are like centaurs that blend into any environment. Their blood-red eyes are on tentacles that protrude from the tops of their oval-shaped heads. Their eyes are also their deadliest weapon. Out of their eyes, the gallops shoot red beams of light that can easily wound any creature. On their faces, where we would expect there to be eyes, are simply two dark indentations. Gallops are oddly colored, too; their upper body, which is humanoid, is olive, while their lower body, the part that looks like a horse, is either brown or white. I hope they don't find us."

Ebeny glanced at the window to make sure nothing was out there.

"Not all of Gorgon's followers are large. Becons look like spaceships the size of dinner plates, but they're not just mindless robots. They are exceedingly intelligent and very good at spying. They can also shoot lasers from their glowing white eyes."

"Yes, I'd agree with that statement," a metallic voice said from a corner of the room. Suddenly, two small, metallic objects flew out from behind the chair where they had been hiding.

Ebeny whispered to Camilla, "Are those becons?"

Camilla nodded, "I think so. Slightly ironic, don't you think?" Ebeny looked over at her sister to see that Camilla's face was pale with fright. Ebeny figured she must look exactly the same, judging from the fear that made her stomach queasy.

Barron stood slowly and moved in front of the sisters to protect them from anything that might happen. "What do you want?"

The becon who had just spoken flew slightly closer and stated with a hint of reverence, "The Last Two." The becons were oval-shaped with lots of flashing lights. One light in particular blinked green whenever they spoke.

"The Last Two? What does that mean, Uncle- uh-Bar-" Ebeny was cut off when the becon continued.

"Do not be frightened, my friends. I am Dy and this is Ga. Gorgon did not send us. We secretly left his legion to warn you. Blackess is not the only evil being who has come for you. Gorgon has sent out a pack of gallops to capture you." The becon seemed to have finished and was looking at Barron expectantly.

The other becon, Ga, ordered, "We need to leave immediately. The gallops could arrive at any moment."

Ebeny and Camilla were stunned. "What?" Ebeny asked. "Leave now?"

"Like this? As we are? Ebeny and I need to take extra clothes or something." Camilla added, eyes wide.

"Go up and pack if you must, but be quick. You have no time to spare," Dy amended.

"What about our school, our friends?" Camilla questioned.

Dy sighed. "You will have to abandon your lives on Earth. I wish there was an easier way for you, but things are happening fast. The sooner we leave, the safer you will be."

"Thank you for warning us, Becons. We are very grateful," Barron said, but he did not move from his defensive position in front of the sisters. He looked at Ebeny and Camilla, who were sitting in stunned silence. "Girls, go and get what you need as quickly as possible."

The girls shakily rose to their feet and walked up the stairs. As Barron sadly looked after them, he missed seeing a flash of olive coming out of the woods.

"I wonder where we are going after we finish packing all this stuff?" Ebeny asked suddenly. "Which shoes should I take? My boots or my sneakers?"

"Oh, I don't know, just pick a pair. Besides we aren't going on a fun vacation, Ebeny. We are going to leave with the becons to go somewhere safe. If we stay here, this could be the last place we ever see. Anyway, you shouldn't be packing all that stuff. We've got to be quick," Camilla said harshly. At twelve years old, Camilla felt it was her job to tell her ten-year-old sister what to do.

Ebeny looked stung at her words. Just then the becons and Barron entered their room. Barron had his own packed bag slung over his shoulder.

"Come on, girls. We *have* to go *now*," he cried, sounding more than a little bit worried.

"Yes," Dy said. "We have no more time. We must leave now if you wish to live or stay out of battle. Not to offend you, but I don't think you have much practice with your magic."

"Magic? We have no magic, at least none that we," she paused to motion at Ebeny and herself, "know of. Unc- ugh, sorry. Barron, do we have magic powers?"

"Grab your things, children, it is time to leave. I saw your horses in the barn out back. Get them and saddle them up. Make sure they have no needs of any kind, and please be careful," Ga instructed the girls and Barron.

"Huh?" Camilla said. "Why horses?"

"We do have a truck you know," Ebeny noted.

Barron turned to look at the girls. "Where we are going, there are no roads and no gas."

"Oh," Camilla stated.

They made their way to the back door. Camilla slowly pushed it open. It squeaked, and she winced, but noticed that nothing was coming around the house.

They then traveled as quickly and quietly as possible to the barn, which was about a hundred yards away from the house. The storm was no longer raging, but a slow drizzle still lingered.

Once inside the barn, they grabbed the bridles and started picking and saddling horses.

"I'm going to take …Apple. I usually ride her," Ebeny announced calmly, as she stroked the appaloosa's spotted nose gently and put the bridle on her.

Camilla looked at Ebeny with a shocked expression. "Ebeny, how can you be so calm? This is life or death here; just pick a horse and let's go," she ordered with a sharp glare, while leading a brown horse out into the open. Ebeny glowered at Camilla.

"Come on, girls. I'll wait for you outside the barn," Barron told the sisters. He had already saddled a golden-brown horse and was leading it to the wide-open door.

"All right," Camilla said and quickly finished saddling Fern. She grabbed the reins and walked out to Barron with Ebeny close behind.

"Let's head back toward the house. We'll wait for the becons by the fence," Barron said. The sisters nodded grudgingly and tugged on the reins to force the horses into movement. Barron took the lead as they neared the house.

In no time, they arrived at the fence and prepared to wait when Ebeny blurted out in a hushed tone, "Wait a minute. I need to go get something." She handed her reins to Camilla and splashed through the puddles to the front door, ignoring Camilla's and Barron's protests. As she got closer to the house, she froze. The front door hung on one hinge with scrapes going up and down it. Instead of a dark yellow door, the paint had been singed and blackened.

Barron and Camilla walked up behind Ebeny after wrapping their horses' reins around a fence post.

"The becons were in there," muttered Barron. Ebeny and Camilla didn't say anything. They simply walked into the house.

Everything was in pieces. They stepped carefully through it all. The bits and pieces of things they owned, and their house—their shattered house.

"What…happened…here?" Ebeny whispered so quietly it was hard to hear.

When she entered the kitchen, she gasped. "Oh. Oh no. Is he…dead?" Lying in front of them was Dy. The becon was smashed, burnt, and torn in half. Ebeny and Camilla looked at each other with sad expressions. They had just met the becon, but they were surprised at how his broken form touched their hearts. Just then Ga zoomed into the room.

"I see you found him. A gallop shot him through with his powerful eye beams. It pains me to see that he died, and I will miss him terribly. I wish you all could have gotten to know him more," Ga paused and looked around at the shattered house then back to the sisters and Barron. "We tried to stop the gallops and convince them that you were already long gone. It worked. They believed us and left, but not before they did all this," Ga sadly said.

"But we weren't gone that long. Look at all this," Ebeny said as she surveyed the damage.

"A pack of gallops can create a lot of destruction in a short amount of time," Barron explained.

"I'm sorry," Camilla told Ga. She felt a surge of sadness for the becon. *He sacrificed quite a lot to save us. This must be hard for him,* Camilla thought and went over to stand beside him. The little family of three stared in silence for a while, their eyes wandering from piece to little piece in misery. Ebeny suddenly ran from the room in search of something. She came back with a small piece of paper in her hands.

Camilla walked over to her and asked her what it was. Ebeny turned it so that Camilla could see. It was the painting of their mother. It was torn at the edges, but no other damage was done.

The girls walked back over to Barron and Ga. Barron hugged the sisters. Neither of them objected, but they both felt a strange distance between themselves and this special person who had just assumed a new identity in their lives. If Barron had kept this immense secret for so long, the sisters wondered how many other secrets he still kept.

After a few heartbreaking moments in silence, they untied their horses, mounted them, and left without a glance back.

As they entered the forest surrounding their house, Barron held out his hand with a small ruby ring on it. A fierce gust of wind blew and then stopped. The surrounding forest turned brighter and different than the one Ebeny and Camilla were used to. It stopped drizzling instantly, and the sun shone through the leaves on the trees. Camilla realized that Barron must have done something, but she didn't know what.

CHAPTER 2

SORIN

It had been two days since they had left their house, and already Ebeny and Camilla were homesick for it. As they rode, Camilla and Ebeny would occasionally glance at Barron's ruby ring. All of their lives they had known him, and he had always worn that ring, but they had never realized what it was for. It was hard to believe that the ring could transport people to a different world in less than a minute. The new world, Zeoch, was beautiful, but it wasn't home.

Ga would make them stop every now and then. It seemed like he was listening for someone or something. After a while, it started to get incredibly annoying.

"This is the hundredth time, Ga! How many more times are you going to make us stop?!" Camilla complained. Her horse was getting agitated, which made her just as nervous.

"I must know if the gallops are near. We becons have hearing that is ten times better than yours, but it helps when silence is all around us. That's why, my dear, I have been stopping so much."

"Oh. I'm sorry. I didn't know. Ebeny and I are still new to all this stuff," Camilla apologized.

"It's all right. Wait, what's that?!" Ga suddenly said. There was a small rustle to their left. Then a small voice piped up.

"Hi. I'm down here. Are you, um, looking for something? I know directions to everything in the woods," the tiny animal said proudly. They stared down at the small creature while he spoke.

The thing looked like an odd bird with a long, furry tail and very small monkey ears that he kept playing with. For a mouth, he had a wide beak that stretched all the way across his face. Except for his tail, he was covered in light brown feathers with a reddish brown stomach. His eyes were a bright hazel color that shone in the sun.

"We know the way to the Enchanted Castle, thank you," Ga told him. He sounded annoyed.

"Ah, yes. You might know a way to get there, but *I* know the best way," the thing said happily.

Ga was about to protest when Barron shot him a warning glance and said, "We'd be happy for you to accompany us, sir."

"Ooooooo, goody! I love going on adventures."

"Excuse me, I don't want to upset you or anything, but what are you exactly?" Ebeny asked, leaning onto Apple's spotted neck. Ebeny was troubled, not knowing what the fast-talking being was. Barron could tell because she only twisted her sleek black hair around her finger when she felt like that.

He chuckled. "Why, I'm a runkey, silly girl. My name is Sorin. Everyone says that I talk a lot. I don't think I do, though. Haven't you ever seen a runkey before? Everyone knows what a run-"

"Please stop your annoying prattle, runkey," Ga interrupted curtly, "These are The Last Two."

"Really? I know who you are," Sorin exclaimed.

"You know us? You're kidding," Camilla said, disbelieving.

"There are well known stories about the two of you. The stories say you will return and save us from Gorgon's reign. Perhaps those stories are true after all," Sorin said with a mysterious tone.

Ebeny asked, "There are *stories* about us?"

Barron stepped forward and told Ebeny calmly, "They are just stories, Ebeny. No one said they were true."

Camilla nodded and added quietly, "It would be cool to save a world, though."

"Yeah," Ebeny agreed.

"I agree, that would be an amazing feeling," Sorin agreed. He abruptly bowed low and as he stood up added brightly, "I must say, though, it is an honor to meet you."

The sisters smiled. Camilla offered, "It's nice to meet you, too. I'm looking forward to having you with us."

The runkey smiled. "I'm so glad we are traveling together, too. Besides," Sorin added, returning to his earlier arrogance, "you'd get lost without me." The sisters laughed, Barron smiled, and Ga sighed. Then he told them, "Okay then. I figure, since we are traveling together, we should be a band. Our band shall be called The Travelers. After all we are *traveling*. Agreed?" They all exchanged puzzled looks. "All right then, I'll take your silence for a yes. The Travelers we shall be."

"Fine, runkey. You may join us while we journey to the Enchanted Castle—preferably in silence," Ga agreed grudgingly.

Sorin glared at him while Camilla and Ebeny stifled giggles.

Barron had told them that the forest they had entered was the Galee Forest. At first, the girls were enchanted with its bright cheerfulness, but the farther the Travelers went, the darker and thicker the forest became. It was very rare when the sun shone through the intertwining branches above their heads. The Galee Forest started to not look or feel that enjoyable anymore. They couldn't even hear the birds sing their wonderful songs. They only heard horse hooves crunching the brown leaves from last fall.

"This is so creepy, guys. I don't know about you, but I'm regretting coming on this trip, or mission, or whatever it is. Although I am glad that I met you, Ga, and Mr. Runkey," Ebeny stated.

"Oh, please, just call me Sorin. It feels like an insult when you call me Mr. Runkey."

"I'm sorry. I didn't know what you preferred to be called."

"My dear Ebeny, it is fine. It was an easy mistake to make," Sorin accepted.

Ebeny sighed in relief and was about to thank Sorin, but a loud rustle made her stop and look ahead in the direction of the sound.

"Shhh," Sorin shushed them quietly. He moved his handwing up and over to point at the patch of tall, thick trees on their left. Then he straightened up and walked over to that spot. When the rest of them showed no signs of moving, he whispered to them, "Move over here. We'll hide till it passes."

The small group quickly joined the runkey and tried to hide as best as they could. Barron and the sisters quickly dismounted their horses and led them behind the tall trees. Then the entire band crouched behind the bushes, even Ga. The rustling got louder, and then they saw it. A gallop. It was exactly like Barron had described. Camilla and Ebeny could clearly see its blood-red eyes on tentacles sprouting from its oval head. Its olive upper body resembled that of a human while everything from its waist down was a brown horse. On its face there were dark indentations where eyes would be. The sisters' eyes widened and they held back a gasp. Camilla glanced at Ebeny and saw she was as surprised as Camilla herself felt. Reaching over, she took her sister's hand and squeezed it tightly before letting go.

The gallop paused and looked around. Camilla hoped it wouldn't discover their hiding place. It continued walking past the hidden group, and Camilla thought they had escaped detection. However, at that moment, Barron's horse snorted and stamped his foot in impatience. Suddenly, the gallop looked over toward them and disappeared.

Ebeny gasped, and then whispered shakily, "Whoa. Did that gallop just disappear? That's impossible, isn't it?"

«Nothing is impossible. After all, you no longer see me, which must mean that I have disappeared,» the gallop's voice emanated out of thin air in front of the sisters.

"Where is that coming from?" Camilla asked.

The gallop reappeared then said, «Ha ha ha. I see you have not yet heard about mynapathy. It is very nice, mynapathy. We gallops don't like verbal communication. We prefer to convey our thoughts through the mind. It is a very convenient way to communicate, especially when you can choose to direct it only to certain people at a time or to everyone at once,» he said mockingly to the band, disappearing again.

"Don't make me shoot my lasers at you, Gallop," Ga warned him menacingly.

«It's hard to hit an unseen target. What will you do when those lasers of yours miss and I retaliate?» The gallop teased. Camilla found it greatly disturbing that she was hearing a voice but couldn't see the speaker. Just then Sorin spoke up from across the clearing.

"Well, sir, we'd love to stay and chat, but we must be on our way," he stated boldly.

«No.» the gallop said and barked out a loud laugh, it sounded forced, more than just laughing.

Then Barron's hand shot out of his dark navy cloak, and a red fire exploded from it. The red fire covered the gallop entirely, momentarily making him visible. In seconds, the fire disappeared, and the gallop was gone, except for a light shadow that hung over the spot. Benny whinnied.

A slight smile appeared on Barron's face as he saw the sisters' amazed expressions. "Didn't think I could do that, did you?" Ebeny and Camilla shook their heads. Barron looked at the rest of the group, nodded, and said, "Let's go now before any more unwanted company shows up." He mounted his horse and headed off through the forest.

Camilla and Ebeny looked at each other in astonishment as they mounted their horses.

"Whoa." Ebeny whispered.

"Tell me about it," Camilla replied quietly. "I was kind of hoping there were no more secrets."

CHAPTER 3

Failure

Gorgon sat on his black, rock throne waiting for Blackess and the gallops to return. He stared defiantly at the door before him with his steel gray eyes, which were a slight shade darker than his ashen skin. Gorgon knew that Blackess and the gallops had gone out only hours before, but it was beginning to feel like days. He tapped his fingers on the arm of his throne to pass the time. The sound echoed in the huge, empty room.

Then finally, when Gorgon was about to lose all of his patience, the door burst open and Blackess staggered across the floor, panting and clutching his gruesome eye. Gorgon smiled as the cowering black beast approached his feet cautiously. His smile soon disappeared when he saw that Blackess was alone.

Glaring down at Blackess, he asked through clenched teeth, "Where…are…the elves…and Barron?" He enunciated each word as sparks from his hands singed the beast's black fur, causing him to yelp.

Blackess bent down even farther at the tone of Gorgon's angered voice. "I…I was unprepared for Barron's actions. I acted cowardly and ran." He removed the hand that was clutching his eye to show Gorgon what had happened. Blackess's once golden eye was now a deep red, and the fur around it was matted with blood. A jagged shard of glass protruded from the damaged eyeball. Gorgon's face was emotionless. Blackess continued, "He did this to me."

"What do you want me to do about it?" Gorgon shouted. "I don't care *what* happens to you now. The bottom line is you *failed*." Blackess yelped as an invisible force grabbed him and lifted his body off the floor. Gorgon growled at the whining creature in front of him and forced the spell to squeeze Blackess tighter and tighter. He didn't stop until Blackess could barely breathe. "Now go to Craammer. He'll remove your eye." As Gorgon snarled the last word, he flung Blackess toward the door. Blackess scrambled to his feet and tore down the hallway, howling as he went.

"Tell the gallops to come in if they are here!" Gorgon yelled after Blackess. In answer to this order, a growl echoed back through the tunnel. He sat back and began to wait once more.

What kind of life am I living now? Gorgon thought as he rested his head against the cool stone and tried to calm down. *My servants can't do what I ask. I should've done it myself.*

The sorcerer sat back and waited. He did not have to wait long; the sound of hoof beats soon reached his ears. He sat up eagerly, hoping that at least the gallops had done something useful and brought back what he had wanted for years.

The gallop pack entered the room slower than Blackess had, but still at a fast pace. Brown and white legs slowed and finally stopped. There was a small ripple in the tightly grouped gallops as they pushed the youngest of them forward.

Gorgon frowned, and the small gallop started to tremble. «Y-your m-majesty,» he stuttered. «W-we d-didn't get what you asked for. Th-they weren't in the house when we got there.» Gorgon clenched his fists in anger and tried to stop the sparks of fire from coming out of his hands.

"Did you follow them?" Gorgon forced out. He clenched his fists tighter, and they began to shake along with the rest of his body.

«W-we went into their home, but they had already left. All we found were two becons. We destroyed one, but the other fled. We went back through the slip and tried to find them, but we couldn't.» The little gallop bent his head in shame and fear.

Gorgon growled and hunched forward. "What am I going to do now? I *need* those three people. I need them now!" he loudly complained. In front of him, the young gallop still hadn't moved.

"Why are you still standing there?" He snarled, and allowed a few red sparks to fly out.

«I-I have a question,» the trembling gallop began. Behind him, Gorgon noticed that the other gallops were trying desperately to get the young gallop's attention. «Why do you w-want those p-people anyway? Did they d-do something to you?»

Gorgon was surprised and impressed by this uncommon show of bravery, but was also infuriated that the young gallop had dared to ask something so personal. "What is your name, gallop?" Gorgon asked, narrowing his eyes.

«G-Grackle, sir.»

"Well, Grackle, didn't your parents ever tell you not to ask me personal questions?" Gorgon demanded, enraged.

«No. My p-parents were killed when I was little,» the gallop answered.

"Don't ever ask me things like that again!" Gorgon hollered. "And you'd better be glad that I didn't kill you on the spot." Grackle bowed his head and backed away quickly into the midst of the other gallops.

"Now go and do not dare return unless you have what I have asked for," Gorgon commanded. The gallops turned and raced out the door.

"Gallops," he muttered under his breath.

As Gorgon sat there in his huge, cold, empty throne room, he tried to force away the painful memories that had been awakened by the curious gallop's question. He remembered how beautiful and breath-taking she was, even on the day she had told him they could never be together and walked away hand-in-hand with Gorgon's enemy. He remembered the safe feeling that always engulfed him when she was near and the jealousy that followed when he saw her with the prince.

"I hate you, I hate you, Barron. You stole away from me the only woman I have ever loved. Now, because of what you've done to me, I will have your head. I will take your daughters' power and use it to destroy you," Gorgon muttered to himself as red sparks flew in every direction. He shook his head to clear his thoughts.

Think, Gorgon, think. Where would he go to protect his priceless daughters? Where … Suddenly a thought struck him. *He would go somewhere he knew there would be help, where a friend lives who can help the elves' powers blossom and where he knows her possessions are.* Gorgon smiled evilly.

"I know where you're going, Barron, you old fool," Gorgon said quietly, as if Barron was standing right in front of him. "I will catch you, and when I do, you'll wish you'd never been born," the sorcerer vowed, letting his red sparks fly.

Gorgon sat back against his chair and let the image of her soft, curly, blonde-streaked red hair; her kind, dazzling blue eyes; and her bright smile fill his head once more.

CHAPTER 4

Elves

After their encounter with the gallop, everyone was quiet and thoughtful. Even Sorin wasn't talking as much as usual, which struck the girls as odd.

Barron gently pulled Benny to a halt. The sisters followed his actions and stopped beside him. "Girls, back at the house, when I was telling you about this world, Zeoch, I never finished because of our quick getaway. What we missed was the most important," Barron added with a serious expression on his face.

"Well, you might find it hard to believe, but everything I'm going to tell you is true."

Ebeny laughed. "Barron, I am now in a world called Zeoch, I'm friends with a talking miniature spaceship and a creature that is a cross between a bird and a monkey, and we survived twice from olive centaur-like creatures. I really don't think there is anything more that can surprise me."

Barron grinned. "All right. Sorin and Ga have been calling you The Last Two because you are the last two elves known to exist from the battle ten years ago."

Ebeny's smile faded. "I take that back. How on earth are we elves? We don't have pointy ears...do we?" Ebeny reached up to feel the tops of her ears just to make sure.

Barron smiled. "Ebeny, this is not a Christmas tale. Elves don't have pointy ears in real life. And to answer your question of how; your mother, Ariona, was an elf." He paused. "Are you ready for another surprise?" Barron asked, his voice lower and gentler. His eyes had an urgent look in them.

Ebeny opened her mouth to speak but Camilla interrupted her. "Ebeny, don't say nothing can surprise you again because we just proved that wasn't possible when Barron said we were . . . elves. Wow, I find that hard to believe." Ebeny shut her mouth and looked to Barron.

"Now that we are home again, I figure it's safe to tell you." Barron took a deep breath and said, "I'm your father." Ebeny and Camilla looked at him with confused anger in their eyes. Barron looked down in shame.

"What? You mean you let us believe for so long we didn't have a father?" A shocked and angry Ebeny yelled at Barron.

"How could you? We had enough trouble without a mom. Couldn't you have at least told us before?" Camilla asked, a little quieter than her sister, but still sounding hurt.

"No, I couldn't. I had to keep the past hidden, or else something far worse could have happened. I didn't like lying to my own daughters, but it was the only thing I could do to keep you safe. I am truly sorry that I let you down," he apologized sincerely with a grave expression. Seeing the pain on his face made Ebeny's anger melt away. She slowly got off her horse and walked over to her new-found father.

"Well, I guess that was a fairly good reason and I guess I can forgive you," Ebeny admitted. She backed off as the tall man dismounted in front of her. He reached out and gave her a hug. Ebeny hugged him back tightly.

As he was hugging Ebeny, Barron looked over to Camilla. She smiled and said softly, "Hi, Dad." Barron smiled.

Barron released Ebeny and announced, "We should go. Daylight doesn't last forever. Let's use it while we have it." He stood and watched her as she mounted her horse. Then he mounted his horse and the group moved onward.

"Uh, Barr— I mean, Dad?" Camilla asked a little after they began moving again.

"Hmmmm," Barron answered.

"Let me get this straight. Our mom was an elf. And you're really our dad? But you're not an elf, right?"

"No. I am a sorcerer. So technically, you are half-elves. But that doesn't make you any less important to the people of Zeoch."

"I still can't believe it. You're our dad. But how would we be in danger if we knew the truth? Why would, oh, what's his name... Gorgon! Why would he want us so badly anyway?" Ebeny asked.

"You are both very strong in many ways, more than you are aware of, which makes you a clear threat to someone as power-hungry as Gorgon. Gorgon and I don't exactly see eye-to-eye either. He would do anything to destroy me and harness your power."

"What? Power? I can't even open a can of olives! I can't be *that* powerful." Ebeny remarked.

Barron fixed Ebeny with a mesmerizing stare. "There are different kinds of power, Ebeny. One day soon you will understand."

Ebeny and Camilla exchanged confused looks. "There's something else," Camilla began awkwardly. "What really happened to our mom? Did she *really* die?"

"I never saw her body, but I think she has to be dead because only death would've kept her away from you this long. Ariona and I went to fight in the battle I told you about earlier but we were separated. Before the battle, we decided that if we lost, then we would take our daughters to the world called Earth and live there until it was safe enough to return to Zeoch. If one of us didn't survive the battle, the other would take our daughters alone. I was devastated when she never returned to our home for I knew I'd have to leave. I wanted to go and search for Ariona and stay in my own world, but I knew that I couldn't. I had to protect you. I had already lost your mother, and I couldn't bear to lose you, too. Once we came out of the slip in space that led to this world, I immediately started trying to cover up our trail and start a new life at the same time."

"A slip in space? You mean the same one we came through the other day?" Camilla asked.

"Yes. But that's not the only one. There are space slips all over the place; you just have to look for them. They don't open unless you have a ring like this made directly by Froghorn himself."

Behind them, a twig snapped. Barron's head whipped around, followed by the girls' and Sorin's. Ga didn't have a head to whip up of his own, but his lights flashed. In front of them stood the gallop who had confronted them earlier. He was leaning against a tree. A ragged gash along his right side was seeping bright red blood.

Barron leapt off his horse with his hands outstretched toward the gallop. His palms were glowing, and sparks were flying out in every direction. Ebeny and Camilla jumped off and stood behind their father on his left side.

«Wait. I have not come to harm you. I wish to make a deal if that is all right with you,» the gallop quickly explained as he held his hands up in a gesture of surrender. Barron put his hands down and stopped advancing toward the wounded gallop, palms no longer glowing, but still shooting sparks to show he was not convinced. The gallop looked past Barron to Camilla and Ebeny.

"Um, why are you looking at us? Are we supposed to decide if we make a deal or not?" Camilla asked the gallop. He nodded and turned to Barron.

"Go on," Barron muttered to his eldest daughter.

"Well, what kind of deal?" Camilla asked.

The gallop pondered this for a moment and then replied. «I wish you to heal my wound, if you can. Then, in exchange, I will help protect you against Gorgon's forces.»

"Why do you need us to heal you? You're all grown up; do it yourself," Ebeny said scornfully.

«I do not have any knowledge of healing, and I am sure you have some supplies in your packs along with an idea of what you'd be doing, young elves. Besides, if I don't get help soon…I fear I will perish.»

Ebeny and Camilla looked at each other. "How do we know that you'll keep your word?" Camilla questioned cautiously.

The gallop raised his hand and tenderly touched his wound, wincing when his finger made contact. Lifting up his bloody finger, he drew a small X over his heart. «I cross my heart and swear to keep my deal.» He looked at the stunned faces of the sisters and said, «It is a gallop's binding mark of true loyalty.»

"Okay, gallop, we will accept your deal," Camilla told the hopeful gallop.

«Thank you.»

Camilla and Ebeny smiled and nodded at the gallop.

There was an odd silence that lasted about a minute. "I think it's time to make camp. Here. Now. Let's go," Sorin ordered the band. Everyone, including the gallop, stared at Sorin. The headstrong runkey shuffled his feet when he realized that he had spoken out of turn.

"That's a good idea, Sorin. Just remember to suggest it and not order it," Barron said. They all laughed quietly, Ga most of all.

As they made camp, Ebeny walked to Camilla and whispered so only she could hear.

"You better know what you are doing. If you don't, it might just cost us our lives, Camilla."

"Yeah, I know," Camilla agreed seriously.

It took about ten minutes to get camp set up. Camilla sat beside the fire and dug out the first aid supplies she was grateful that she had thought to throw into her bag before they left home. The gallop sat quietly beside her, waiting. As the others were trying to get comfortable in their makeshift beds of leaves and moss, Barron came over to Camilla. He bent down and asked, "Do you need any help?"

Camilla smiled and replied, "Yeah, thanks, Dad." It still sounded strange calling him "Dad." Together they worked to clean the wound as Barron held the gallop still and Camilla wiped away the dried blood. Soon, Barron and Camilla had bandaged the wound.

"Thanks again, Dad," Camilla said. "You can go to sleep now. I just want to put another bandage around him and clean up the supplies." Camilla hoped he agreed. She desperately wanted to be alone with the gallop to ask him why he would want to help Ebeny and herself. Barron had said that gallops work for Gorgon.

Barron sighed. "Okay. Camilla, just make sure you're careful," he relented. Barron hugged her and walked over to a nearby tree and sat at its base, watching them carefully. Camilla began to carefully wrap another bandage tighter over the wound. Her long chestnut-colored hair rippled in the faint wind. She was about to ask the gallop a question when he began to speak.

«Thank you. I mean, for saying that you would help me. That meant a lot to me. I know it seems odd that I'm saying this to you, but I am not like the other gallops. My friends and mother would not approve of my even talking to you. I have been trained from a young age to kill humans and elves, not befriend them.» He paused, as if he was deciding whether to continue. Finally, he did.

«At Galvis, my home, I longed to avenge my father's death. He was killed when I was four years old. I believed he was killed by elves. But recently, I found out the truth. My father died because he was trying to protect an elf named Ariona and a sorcerer named Barron. That man over there.» The gallop nodded toward Barron, who was still staring at them intently. «And he died trying. My mother killed him. It broke my heart to hear that. But I know it's the truth. I overheard a conversation that was not meant for me. My mother still doesn't know that I know. Now I want to be like my father. I want to protect the elves.» He paused and seemed to cry with his eyes.

"Oh, it's okay, gallop. I know what it feels like. My, um, dad lied to me. He said that he was Uncle James, but was he? No. No, he wasn't my uncle," Camilla whispered. She was trying to make him feel better.

«Thank you for trying to make me feel better. My name is Poot, runaway of Galvis.»

Camilla finished dressing the wound and began to pack up the supplies.

«You did a good job on my wound. Where did you learn to do that?»

"Bar—I mean Dad had Ebeny and I take a first aid class a few months ago. He said it would come in handy some day, and I guess he was right. I'm not a doctor, but I hope this will keep you alive until we find help," Camilla answered.

«Once again, thank you very much. I hope that your sister will like me once she gets to know me.» The gallop said to her.

"She will. Don't worry about it," Camilla said. "Poot, if you want to protect elves, like you said, why did you threaten us in the forest?"

«I sensed that there was another gallop pack around listening to our conversation. I had to lie and make the other gallops think I had captured you. Once they thought I had you cornered, I sensed that they had left. If I had not done what I did, you might have been caught then and there,» Poot explained.

"Oh. Well, then, thank you," Camilla said as she got up and walked over to Ebeny's shelter by a rather large oak, hoping to tell her all about her strange conversation with Poot, the gallop, but Ebeny was already asleep, cozy on her bed of leaves and moss under the bright, shining stars in the dark sky above them.

Sighing in disappointment, Camilla dragged herself over to her own shelter that was underneath the leafy branches of a tall maple tree. She was so exhausted that she fell asleep instantly.

Barron had overheard almost every word that the gallop, Poot, had said. He was still unsure of whether he could trust him or not. Barron's eyes watched the gallop closely until he knew that he had fallen asleep. Only then did Barron allow his eyes to shut.

CHAPTER 5

The Enchanted Castle

It was bright and early when Ebeny awoke the next day. She wasn't wearing a watch, so she didn't know exactly what time it was. When her eyes were open, she had to hold down a gasp. In front of her was the wounded gallop.

"Good morning, Ebeny. Did you sleep well?" Camilla asked her calmly. She had stopped trying to make the gallop stand still so she could gently wipe off the dried blood that covered his wound like a casing. Ebeny looked on the ground around the gallop. A scarlet bandage lay in a crumpled heap on the ground.

«Good morning,» the gallop greeted her as well.

"Hello, Ebeny," Sorin said from a tree at the edge of the clearing.

"This is Poot. He ran away from Galvis, a gallop village. Last night he told me his story. It's sad. Poot's mother killed his father because he was trying to protect *our* mother and father," Camilla informed her.

"What? He's a good guy? That doesn't make sense," Ebeny stammered, her gaze darting from her sister, to the gallop, and back again.

"Will you come over here and help me? The others are off looking for some more food. Dad and I put a bandage on Poot's wound last night, but blood is still seeping out." It sounded as if she were begging her to help. Silently Ebeny got up and went over to help her struggling sister.

"I believe that we are doing the right thing, but doesn't it seem odd that the first time we do first aid on someone it is a creature that we've never seen before?" Ebeny asked Camilla.

"Yeah," Camilla agreed. She handed Ebeny a few clumps of moss. "Here. Use these to help stop the bleeding. We don't have any gauze pads left, just wrap, and we can't use that." Ebeny nodded and took the moss clumps. Gently, she held them onto Poot's wound.

«Ouch!» Poot complained.

"Sorry!" Ebeny said quickly.

The girls managed to wrap a bandage around the wound that seemed to stop the bleeding for now.

«I feel awful,» Poot said. «But I do think that the bandages helped a little.»

Ebeny and Camilla smiled. "Thanks, Poot," they said together.

As they were cleaning up, a voice from behind startled them. "We caught two small leets and a zarsk. It will take a while to prepare a meal, but I believe that we can pass the time quite easily," Barron announced.

"Two leets and a zarsk?" Ebeny asked. "Look like two squirrels and a buck to me."

"They are similar creatures," Barron agreed. He sat down by a pile of leaves and twigs to start the fire. "So, Camilla, would you like to share the story behind our friend here? I overheard last night, but I don't think that everyone else did," Barron prodded as he got a small, but hot fire going. She hesitated and looked over at Poot. He nodded, so she explained to them.

"Well to start, his name is Poot, runaway from Galvis, his old home. But anyway, he was not like other gallops. He was like his father," And with lots of questions, Camilla told the story of her new friend Poot.

Everyone listened very closely. As she finished Poot's story, they all had a deep respect for him.

"So. You're the son of the gallop who tried to save us from the governor of Galvis's ambush. I thought you looked familiar. But I wasn't sure. You can't be too careful these days. I'm sorry for the amount of pain I caused you," Barron apologized sincerely.

Ebeny and Camilla looked at Barron quizzically. "I suppose you'd like to know more about that, right?" Barron asked them. The girls both nodded, so he continued. "Well, Poot's father's name was Brenas. We became best friends at a very young age. Luckily, Gorgon didn't influence the gallops like he does today or our friendship would never have happened. We grew into adulthood together. It was during that time, however, that Gorgon began recruiting the gallops. Gorgon had said that the gallops would be fighting for a great and noble cause. Brenas's father agreed to fight for Gorgon. Brenas didn't want to let his father down, so he joined, too. The next year the war began. It was unfortunate that Brenas was such a good soldier because he was chosen to lead many battles that I lead as well. We avoided each other as much as we could, but that didn't always work." Barron took a deep breath and closed his eyes before continuing with his story.

"Brenas had a wife," he said softly as he reopened his eyes. "She truly believed in Gorgon's cause and killed many of the king's army. She knew that Brenas and I were still friends and she despised him for it. During one of the battles, Ariona and I were back to back fighting for our lives. My sword was knocked out of my hands and Ariona's sword as well. We began using magic but it zapped our energy. Suddenly, Brenas jumped out from our attackers and saved our lives. He surprised them which gave us enough time to grab our swords, but this time, Brenas fought with us. Somewhere else in the battle, his wife saw him, and she galloped over to us. As she broke through the circle of Gorgon's army that surrounded Brenas, Ariona and me, her eyes came alight and she shot her heat beams straight at Brenas. The beams hit him square in the chest. Brenas dropped to the ground, and I knelt next to him. Ariona later told me that I cried, but I have no memory of it. I held him close to me, but soon Gorgon's forces recovered from the shock of one of their own soldiers killing an ally and attacked again." Again Barron paused. He took a shaky breath and his eyes became hard, his voice angry. "I ran after his wife but couldn't catch her. I was filled with rage." He scared them all when red sparks came out of his hands.

"I'm sorry. That happens when I get angry, but since the Earth world didn't let me use any magic whatsoever, I forgot all about it," Barron said.

«I knew that's what happened. I knew it!» Poot shouted with a combination of sorrow and satisfaction.

"Excuse me," Ga said. "I believe this meat that I have been frying is now done. Come and get some."

"Ooooo!" Ebeny shouted. "Me first, me first!"

They kept riding for three, long days, only stopping to sleep, get water, and get food. They redid Poot's bandages quite often; the movement of walking was making the slightly red bandages slip off. No one talked except a small whisper to his or her horse or a small grunt from Poot about his wound.

Then finally on the fourth day they arrived at their destination.

"Oh! It's beautiful!" "Look at the towers and moat!" "What an amazing castle!" Camilla and Ebeny shouted in turn.

"Yes, my dears. It is the Enchanted Castle! With many great wonders just waiting for you," he answered excitedly.

Ebeny gazed up in awe at the tall castle in front of her. She noticed a tan figure disappearing inside a door above the front gate. She stared after him, but decided to say nothing about it to the others.

The castle was made of marble. All the towers had shining jewels on the tops. The watch tower was the most marvelous. It was made of what looked like pure silver that reflected magnificent colors in the sun's light.

They rode their horses over the huge, wooden drawbridge which led them through an elaborate archway on the other side of the moat. The arch itself was white and had a black detailed outline of a butterfly in the middle with the words; FREEDOM AND CHANGE from one end to the other in big block letters. *Wow, what a place,* Ebeny thought, exhilarated. *I would like to live in a place with freedom and change. It's also so beautiful here!* They traveled down a glimmering corridor filled with life-size stone statues every few feet. The corridor opened into a large courtyard brimming with multi-colored flowers. In the middle of the courtyard sat a shimmering marble fountain. The floor glistened with magically changing colors in different patterns that shifted constantly.

Suddenly, a tall man strode out from amidst the flowers. He was a slender person with jet black hair and dark violet eyes. His skin was dark and his black hair was done in small braids tight to his head that stopped at the base of his neck and continued loosely to his shoulders. White teeth made up a large smile that lit up his face. He wore long robes made of light blue satin. His shoes were dark blue moccasins decorated with tiny, brightly colored beads.

"Hello, visitors to the Enchanted Castle. I am King Shamoola and am overjoyed to have guests in my castle," the man called Shamoola explained. He looked at Barron and said, "Welcome back, old friend."

"Good to see you," Barron replied, dismounting his horse. He reached out and shook Shamoola's hand. Turning to the girls, he said, "Shamoola and I have been friends for many years."

Shamoola looked at the three horses and clapped his hands loudly. From off to their right scurried a short man with large feet and hands but a tiny head. "Please take our guests' horses and put them in the stable," King Shamoola ordered. The short man nodded and waited patiently for Ebeny and Camilla to dismount their steeds before leading them away through the surrounding gardens.

Shamoola turned back to the group and gasped when he caught sight of Poot. "My dear fellow, what in heaven's name happened to you? That is a most serious wound and we must get you to the infirmary straight away. Follow me!"

«Thank you, Your Majesty,» Poot said, following slowly behind the king. Barron and the girls followed with Sorin and Ga in the rear.

King Shamoola led them through the courtyard, weaving through the plants until they arrived at a big door that was engraved with many designs. Shamoola rapped twice on the door with a big knocker and it opened with a creak. He led them through, and the door closed behind them.

The group entered a large, octagonal room that was brightly lit from a glass chandelier hanging from the ceiling. It was as if they had entered a beehive. Lots of people and creatures were entering and leaving through eight different massive oak doors.

All of the people they passed looked startled, but they didn't say anything. The small group went through one of the doors on their left, which opened onto a small, crowded hallway. They traveled on, not knowing what to expect next.

CHAPTER 6

You're Fixed!

Soon after entering the hallway, King Shamoola led the group through a smaller door. When everyone was through the door, Shamoola took them down a long brightly lit hallway where the smell of food found its way to their nostrils.

They passed an open door and looked inside. There were ten big tables lined in rows of five with silver cups, plates, forks, and spoons. Red and violet tablecloths had been placed on the tables. Two tall chairs sat at the front of the room with a table in front that had gold silverware and a blue tablecloth.

It's so beautiful! I wonder if we will get to eat in there? Ebeny thought as Shamoola led them away from the glorious smells and sights.

"Well, here we are," he announced. They had come into a large room with fifteen beds and each one had a different design on the sheets. Only five of the beds were occupied with patients. Four nurses bustled around in crisp white uniforms.

Shamoola led the group over to an unoccupied bed and gently assisted Poot down onto the bed. He told the rest of them to wait a bit while he went to get a healer and disappeared behind a curtain. The sisters shared a confused look, but said nothing. Behind them the curtain ruffled as Shamoola emerged leading a tall man in a tan cloak over to Poot's bed.

The healer quietly walked over to Poot and examined his wound. Poot quickly explained what had happened. The healer nodded and walked over to Ebeny and Camilla.

"Do you care for your friend?" the healer asked. Ebeny and Camilla nodded. "Hmm, that is good," the healer responded. He walked back over to Poot and pulled a small bag out of his robe. Bending over the injured gallop, he reached into the bag. His hand emerged with a pinch of light peach colored powder. While murmuring words indistinguishable to Ebeny's and Camilla's ears, the healer sprinkled the powder in a circular motion over the gash. Everyone held their breath, hoping for the best, as the healer stood up,.

Ebeny and Camilla gasped. The once open and bleeding gash along Poot's side was slowly closing together. Within a minute, the wound was completely healed.

«Why, thank you,» Poot said, clearly as surprised as the sisters were. The healer merely bowed slightly and disappeared behind the curtain.

"Wow, that powder must be really magical. There's hardly even a scar!" Ebeny stated. Camilla nodded.

"It's amazing," Sorin added.

"It is a good thing we came here, or it may have taken weeks for that to heal," Ga remarked.

"It is not just the magic in the powder, but the hope and love of others around that does the trick," Shamoola explained. "It would not have worked as well if you all hadn't been hoping for him to be healed. Hope, love, and trust can be stronger than even the most powerful spell." Ebeny nodded and vowed she'd never forget those words.

Poot began to get off the bed, but Shamoola reached out and put a hand on his chest to stop him. "You can't go just yet. You'll need to stay here for a few hours to make sure there is no infection as a result of your injury," the king said.

Poot nodded, «Whatever is necessary.»

Once everyone was sure Poot was all right, the group headed out of the hospital. Shamoola ordered a guard to escort them to their rooms.

Once out of the hospital, the guard said his name was Zimi. Zimi told the weary group as they began walking, "Mr. Sorin, you will be sharing a room with Sir Barron. I hope this is not an inconvenience for either of you."

"It would be a great pleasure to room with Barron, someone who actually wanted me to join you on your journey to this castle," Sorin said with a sharp look at Ga.

"And I would enjoy Sorin's company very much," Barron added with a smile.

Zimi bowed. "Wonderful. Mr. Ga, you will be staying in your own room. I strongly hope that this doesn't displease you."

One of Ga's lights blinked orange and he replied. "I would not ask you to change a thing for me."

Zimi bowed once more and led the Travelers down two halls, then stopped at an enormous staircase. *Wow! What a beautiful staircase!* Ebeny thought. The railing was gold and silver with little scattered gems embedded in the surface. The stairs themselves were the color of rubies with a long, violet velvet rug laid on them. The long rug had a border of bright yellow silk. The staircase was so dazzling that they couldn't imagine anything more beautiful.

But they had not seen their rooms yet

CHAPTER 7

Rooms and a Box

Barron and Sorin's room was a book-lover's paradise. Barron nodded to Zimi with a smile as the guide held the door open for Barron and Sorin to pass through. Bookshelves lined every wall, and every shelf was bursting with every kind of book imaginable. Barron immediately walked to the shelves and began to peruse the books. There was also a large circular table in the middle of the room. It had stacks of paper and quills in ink bottles. Barron's large bed was along the far wall beside a desk. The sheets and pillows had many colors, and the quilt had a diamond shaped pattern of green and blue.

"Wow, that's a lot of books," Ebeny commented.

"Yeah, really. How are you going to know which to read first?" Camilla wondered.

Barron shrugged. "I'll probably just close my eyes and pick one."

Ebeny nodded. "I guess that's pretty efficient."

In a corner of the room was a nest sitting in a makeshift tree with a small, hovering table, on which sat a bowl of what looked like mashed bananas and bugs. Ebeny and Camilla were clearly disgusted. Sorin looked at the sisters and said, "Don't wrinkle your noses. I assure you, that this is quite tasty. Would you like to try it?"

"Yeah, I'll try it, Sorin. I'll try it...when pigs fly!" Ebeny said. Everyone chuckled.

Barron and Sorin stayed in their room as Zimi led the sisters and Ga down the hall to another room. Arriving at a smaller door, Zimi opened it and bowed to Ga. "Is this Ga's room, Zimi?" Camilla asked.

"Yes," Zimi replied simply.

Ga's room was much different than Barron's. It was a square room, about fifteen feet wide. A table sat against a wall just under an outlet. The walls were a deep orange color that had paintings of the past on them. A single window was the only source of light.

"But there's nothing here!" Ebeny said, surprised.

Ga zoomed around the room and then sighed contentedly. Turning back to Ebeny he said, "It is all I need." Ebeny shrugged in acceptance and followed Zimi and Camilla up a short flight of stairs.

They reached a tall door with a bronze knob. Zimi bowed and opened the door.

"What do you think?" Zimi asked as they entered the room.

"Oh wow, Zimi!" Camilla smiled and exclaimed happily, "It's...it's magnificent!"

Vibrant colors decorated the room. Dazzling lamps sat on three tables, two bedside tables and one table in the middle of the circular room. Book shelves filled with glorious fantasy and history novels stood on the right side of the room. There were four windows in the room that offered amazing views. The window panes were made of silver and the curtains looked like gold. Three shining oak desks covered with more books and writing utensils sat beside the bookshelves. A wonderful glass chandelier glowed with bright yellow light. Two neatly made beds sat in different corners of the room. The pillows were velvet and the bed sheets were satin. Both pillows and sheets were dark red and stood out against the cool colors of the rest of the bed. Long silk canopies framed each bed. The quilts and canopies on the beds were many shades of green and blue.

"You may unpack now or wait till after the feast. It is your choice," Zimi explained.

"What?" Camilla questioned.

"A feast? Where?" Ebeny asked.

"It's in your honor and is being held in the dining hall," Zimi explained.

"You mean that amazing room we passed earlier that smelled like delicious food?" Ebeny asked.

Camilla rolled her eyes. "No, Ebeny. The room that we passed is actually a closet even though it has rows of tables set for dinner and smells curiously of food."

Ebeny laughed. "Point taken," she accepted.

Zimi smiled at the sisters before answering Ebeny's question. "Yes. The room we passed is the dining hall and we'll be eating there. You may wish to change before going to the feast. If so, this room used to house a young lady a few years ago, so there are many outfits in the closet and other things in the dressers." Zimi motioned to the door on their left. "I hope you like them, and I'll see you at the feast.," Zimi bowed and walked out of the room.

"Okay, bye! Thanks!" Camilla called after him.

"What a room, Camilla! Isn't it terrific?!"

"Yes it is, Ebeny."

It was like Christmas. Every time they picked up another book, it filled them with new knowledge and joy. When they opened the closet in the corner, they discovered wonderful dresses and shoes, just as Zimi had said. Opening a large drawer, their eyes looked over beautiful jewelry of all kinds. Camilla remembered Zimi had told them they could wear whatever was in the closet and dressers. Camilla stepped into the closet and picked out a dress and some shoes. Then, going back to the dresser, she found some jewelry that matched and went into the large bathroom Ebeny had discovered to get ready. Following her example, Ebeny took a few things as well and stepped into the bathroom after her sister had exited.

When the sisters had finally finished, they looked at themselves in a full length mirror with silver trim. A huge, shiny diamond sat on top of the mirror. The bright sun shone down on the girls through a window and made their sparkly dresses light up in an array of red and pink. They slid their just washed feet into their matching shoes Each girl had her hair pulled back tightly in a bun. As Ebeny inspected her image in the mirror, she noticed something in the back corner.

"Hey, what's that box with the freaky writing on? It's glowing red." Ebeny twisted to point her finger at what she was talking about.

"What are you…" Camilla trailed off as she followed Ebeny's guiding finger. The wooden box was indeed glowing bright red with strange writing on it and odd symbols that looked oddly familiar. She wondered where she had seen it before.

"Hold on, I think I can read that. Can you, Ebeny?" Ebeny nodded slowly. "It says, 'To open this box, you must find the key. Peer into the crystal, and you will see.' Well, that's really weird. How about we don't worry about it right now."

"I think you're right, Camilla." Ebeny said with her eyes still glued to the box. "Do you know what's even stranger than this box?"

"What?"

"The fact that we just read this writing without even hesitating. How did we do that?"

A knock at the door interrupted their thoughts. Camilla hurried over and opened the door.

She smiled. "Hey, Poot! How are you?" Camilla asked the gallop.

«I am perfectly fine. Shamoola had said to meet him at the dining hall when I got out of the infirmary. When I met Shamoola in the dining hall, he sent me to retrieve you two. It is time for the feast. Shamoola wishes you to walk down with him,» Poot told them. Ebeny joined Camilla by the door.

"Sure, Poot," Ebeny said.

«Now please come if you will. I can take you to Shamoola and we'll all go down together.»

"Okay, we're coming. We just have to shut these closet doors. Oh, and by the way, you look much better," Ebeny told Poot, much to his surprise.

«Why, thank you, Ebeny. You look very nice, too.» The sisters smiled and blushed slightly as they followed their friend out of the room.

CHAPTER 8

Party Crashers

"You look lovely tonight, girls! I'm glad you found everything you needed." Ebeny and Camilla had just met Shamoola at the top of the stairs King Shamoola was wearing a white suit that fit him perfectly. His tie was a dark blue with a butterfly, much like the one on the arch that they had seen when entering the castle. Shining white dress shoes completed the outfit nicely. His hair was no longer in braids but pulled back in a low ponytail.

"Why, thank you, King Shamoola. Now let's get to that feast. I don't know about you, but I'm starving," Ebeny remarked. Camilla nodded.

"You are very welcome. Yes, dear, we are going to the feast and please, just call me Shamoola. We should get going. Barron, Ga, and Sorin are already there. They said that they could handle things until I arrive but I'm not so sure," Shamoola explained with a smile.

"Okay, Shamoola," Camilla said. Shamoola led them down many beautiful hallways. All of the halls were empty, for everyone was eating at the feast. Ebeny and Camilla could hear laughter and talking from the end of the corridor that got louder as they neared the dining hall. Finally, Ebeny could see the dining area and the long, wonderfully decorated tables that she had seen earlier.

As they entered the dining hall, a silence fell over the room as if the diners were in a trance. The clacking sound of Poot's hooves echoed in the quiet of the room. Ebeny searched the tables and immediately found Barron, Sorin, and Ga already seated at the head table. Camilla and Ebeny looked at each other and quickly hurried over to Barron's table and sat down on either side of him. Barron gave his daughters a warm smile, and they returned it to him. Poot trotted over to stand beside Camilla.

"Good citizens of the Enchanted Castle, thank you all for coming to our feast this grand evening to welcome our guests," Shamoola announced as he turned and gestured at the table where Ebeny, Camilla, and Poot had just seated themselves beside their companions. A loud chorus of claps and hollers of excitement followed the king's words. Shamoola calmly raised his hands, and the silence returned. "Now that we have finally arrived," he added with a wink directed at the sisters, "You may feast!" He bowed deeply, and the noise started up again as everyone dug into the food.

Ebeny looked around her at the unusual food. The dishes of food were nothing like on Earth, and Ebeny found herself hesitant to try any of it. Slowly, she reached forward and spooned purple cream onto her plate followed by a slice of an orange square and a few chunks of what she recognized as some kind of meat similar to zarsk. The rest of the food looked too strange for Ebeny to attempt to try. She picked up a gold spoon, dipped it into the purple cream, and then put the spoon into her mouth. This first mouthful of food was like an explosion of irresistible, smooth sweetness that reminded her of black raspberry ice cream and chocolate pudding rolled into one. Her eyes widened as she immediately swallowed, picked up her spoon, and shoved more into her mouth.

"Wow," Ebeny said through a mouthful of the purple pudding. "This stuff is really good!" Beside her, Camilla nodded, her eyes bright. On Camilla's plate were two triangle shaped yellow fluffy cookies, a pile of tiny white circles that resembled rice, and some of the zarsk.

"Yeah, I thought it would be disgusting and that I wouldn't like it, but this stuff is *amazing*!" Camilla agreed enthusiastically.

Barron laughed. "I knew you'd like it, but I didn't think you'd turn into crazed food monsters when you ate it!" Ebeny and Camilla blushed deeply and turned away. Barron's voice softened as he added, "But I guess I'm as much of a food monster as you." He picked up the leg he was eating and took a huge bite out of it. Ebeny and Camilla glanced at him and had to start laughing. Sauce was dripping down his chin, and his cheeks bulged from the amount of food. Poot and Sorin looked over and began to laugh, too.

Ebeny smiled and picked up something small, round, and yellow from in front of her and thought gleefully, *This is the best day ever. Nothing could happen to dampen my spirit!*

Suddenly off to Ebeny's right, a loud *boom* echoed through the hall, followed by the clatter of rocks and several terrified screams.

Everyone stood and looked toward the noises. Out of an enormous hole in the wall, many gallops and other fearsome creatures leaped into the dining hall. When the dinner guests realized what was happening, everyone in the hall panicked and began to run toward the door leading to the rest of the castle. Poot, Ga, and Shamoola ran against the pull of the crowd toward the newly opened hole in the wall. Barron paused just long enough to say to Ebeny and Camilla, "Go back to your room. I'll meet you there," before he, too, raced off in the direction of the hole.

"What's going on?!" Ebeny shouted. She grasped Camilla's hand tightly and looked to her for reassurance, but Camilla looked just as scared as Ebeny was.

"I don't know," Camilla answered, doing her best to sound calm. "But we have to get back to our room. That's what Dad told us to do, remember?" Ebeny nodded. She stood up, with Camilla's hand still in hers, and ran.

They jumped down from the ledge that the head table rested on and raced toward the door. The sisters ran into the tide of frantic feast guests and were pulled along with them.

Behind them, the sisters heard hoof beats getting louder and closer. Suddenly, two gallops emerged from the crowd behind them. Ebeny and Camilla began to run faster, but the gallops wrapped their arms around the girls and lifted them off the ground. The sisters tried to escape, but their kidnappers' grips were pure iron. The gallops headed toward the opening in the wall. Ebeny and Camilla locked eyes, and Ebeny could see her own terror reflected back at her in Camilla's gaze.

"Ah ha!" came a high-pitched voice from above the sisters. Suddenly, a silver spoon from one of the tables hit Ebeny's captor on one of his eye tentacles. In astonishment, the gallop loosened his grip just enough for Ebeny to kick free. Ebeny dropped to the ground and looked up to see Sorin hovering by a chandelier armed with two more spoons. She scrambled to her feet as the gallop grabbed at her again, but before he could catch her, two more spoons bounced off the gallop's head in quick succession. "Gotcha again! Ha ha, don't mess with the silver spoon master!" Sorin shouted with glee.

The gallop glared at Sorin, but before he had time to retaliate, the sound of a horn reverberated throughout the hall. The gallop hesitated for a few seconds before galloping away towards the hole where Barron, Shamoola, and Poot had been holding back the remaining horde of monsters.

"Ebeny!" Camilla screamed. Ebeny turned and saw her sister struggling in the arms of the gallop who was whisking her away toward the opening in the wall. Ebeny immediately took off after her sister.

Over by the hole, Barron shot yet another ball of fire at a scaly multi-legged creature that collapsed on the spot. Behind the creatures he was fighting, Barron saw a gallop carrying Camilla toward the hole in the wall. He growled with anger and pushed at his enemies. He swung quicker at the creatures, desperate to get through them to his daughter, but the horde pushed him back farther and farther from the escaping gallop.

Shamoola and Poot saw this, too, but they were pushed back as well. Barron cried out in anguish as he watched his struggling daughter disappear through the hole in the arms of her captor.

The gallop nimbly jumped away from the castle with Camilla yelling angrily at him, "Put me down! Put me down NOW!!!"

The gallop who was holding her simply replied, «No, no. Gorgon wants *needs* to see you,» Then he started laughing in such a cruel way that made Camilla stop talking and simply looked back at the castle with terror-filled eyes.

«Don't think your little friends will save you. They aren't even good trackers! My bet is that you won't see your family back there again for the rest of your pathetic life.»

The gallop held his captive tighter as he and his revolting band of creatures raced through the dark of night and into the surrounding forest. They left the Enchanted Castle far behind.

Back in the feast room, Ebeny stood in the rubble, looking out of the gaping hole and into the night and wept for her lost sister.

"Camilla! You can't leave me. You can't." Ebeny's tears streamed down her face.

Barron moved up behind Ebeny and wrapped his arms tightly around her. He could feel her shaking as she cried. He himself felt like crying with his daughter, but Barron held back.

A horrifying thought echoed through Ebeny's head. *She's gone. What on earth am I going to do without her?* At the same time, miles away, a little elf girl, held captive in a gallop's arms, thought the same awful thing.

CHAPTER 9

Gorgon's hope

Gorgon paced the floor of his throne room. He wondered if he should've trusted the gallops to capture the elves again, in spite of their first failure. Gorgon stopped pacing and turned toward the door. His patience had run out. He walked briskly toward the door and then down the long hallway.

The hallway was lit with small torches. The fire was a vibrant blue that made the stone walls glow eerily. On the sides of the hall hung portraits of Gorgon himself that were done by the best painters from all over Zeoch.

Gorgon walked briskly past the paintings without a glance and soon stormed out into the main room. He paused just long enough to admire a tall silver statue of himself. Then he strode up to the enormous oak doors. He grabbed the sizable brass handles and pulled the doors wide open.

He walked out into the gloomy haze that surrounded his castle. Walking out farther, Gorgon felt a cool breeze. He stopped moving at the top of the stone steps. He peered into the misty surroundings for any sign of movement.

I might as well sit here and wait for the messenger. The cool wind might calm me down, Gorgon thought gloomily. He lowered himself down onto the cold rock steps and prepared to wait anxiously yet again.

Gorgon was soon surprised. Out of nowhere, a gallop burst from the heavy fog and headed straight for Gorgon at top speed.

«Gorgon!» the gallop called out. «Gorgon! General Shale has sent me with news.» The gallop skidded to a stop right in front of Gorgon.

"What is it then? Come on, spit it out!" Gorgon commanded. He could hardly contain his excitement.

«General Shale broke into the Enchanted Castle and has successfully captured one of the elves. He-» Gorgon cut him off.

"What do you mean *one* of the elves. I need both of them. And what about Barron? You didn't get him?" Gorgon snarled. He was glad that he had at least *one* of the elves, but he needed both of them and Barron.

«I'm sorry, My Lord. The mynapathy message I received did not say what happened to the others,» the gallop explained uneasily.

"Fine," Gorgon said, trying hard to control his temper. "Where are they now?"

«On their way, sir. General Shale said that he would bring the elf to you so you wouldn't have to ride all the way out there.»

Gorgon was about to reply when a thought suddenly popped into his head. He grinned wickedly. "Good. Wonderful. This is perfect. The other elf and Barron will come searching for the one we have. When they reach my castle, I will capture all of them. Then, I will kill Barron," Gorgon laughed. "And I'll soon have those elves' power. They will have no choice but to join me," Gorgon told himself gleefully.

«Um, sir?» the gallop asked tentatively. «What will you do if the elves, uh, refuse to join you?»

Gorgon glared at the gallop with an evil glint in his eyes. A humorless smile formed on his lips and turned his face into a terrifying mask. "I will eliminate them."

CHAPTER 10

her Only friend

It had been a few hours since Camilla had been captured. Camilla's mind was torn with thoughts that popped into her head. *Am I really an elf? Will I ever see my family again? Will I survive?* She had never felt so overwhelmed and confused. Camilla looked about her and noticed that they were slowing down.

«Little elf, we are stopping for camp. Go find a place to lie down in that nearby cave,» a booming mynapathy voice ordered her. «Just don't think of escaping; we have eyes everywhere.»

Camilla stumbled over to the mouth of the cave. She shuffled into the cool cave and leaned against the wall. The cave was tiny, but it was better than being outside among all the frightening beasts. She took one look around her, slumped on the ground in misery, and quickly slipped back into her anguished thoughts.

After what seemed to Camilla like only seconds a voice, kind of like a hiss, sounded from the cave entrance. "Prizzzziner, come here, Sssshale wantssss to talk to you." She looked to her right, in the direction of the voice. In front of her stood the oddest looking thing with crab claws and a snake body. Black, beady little eyes stared down at her. Just as it did, the rest of the camp got quiet.

"Fffollow me. No trouble now, little elfff." He slithered away from the entrance of the cave, and Camilla slowly got up and followed him. "Now, lissssten up, when you addressss Sssshale use the words *ssir* or *general.*" He stopped and turned around to face her. "Isss that clear?"

"What does this Shale want with me?"

"Ssstop asssking ssssilly questionsss. It'ssss General Sssshale."

Camilla looked in front of her. A tall gallop with a lower body so dark that it was almost black was standing there. He had broader shoulders and bigger, more noticeable muscles than the other gallops. His eyes were cold and pure evil. «Little elfling, tell me your name. And, please don't try to trick me.»

"My name? Don't you even know who you captured?" Camilla pretended to look surprised.

«I know very well whom I've captured. I've captured a little elfling who will regret it if she doesn't cooperate and answer my questions. Now tell me your name.» His eyes glowed red, and Camilla remembered Barron's description of gallops shooting lasers from their eyes, so she decided to play it safe.

"My name is Camilla, sir."

«That's better,» General Shale said. «I want to warn you not to use your magic against us. If you did, I'm afraid it would end badly. My orders are to deliver you to Gorgon alive, but that doesn't mean you have to be in perfect condition.»

Camilla gulped and stared at him dumbfounded. "What magic?" she asked.

«Don't insult me. I know all about your magical powers.» The muscular gallop glared at her.

Camilla remained silent.

«I'll interpret your silence as obedience. You may go. Tracker, my faithful bambargle, will escort you back to your sleeping quarters.»

The bambargle nodded and nudged Camilla with his claw. They walked slowly back to the small cave.

"Have a good ssssleep. I'll be watching you."

Camilla made her way to the back of the cave in an attempt to get as far away from the frightening captors as she could. "Home sweet home," she said sarcastically. *Home. I miss home. More than anything, I miss my dad and Ebeny. I even miss Sorin, Ga, Poot, and Shamoola.* She sighed forlornly.

Suddenly, a strange rustling noise came from the bushes at the mouth of the cave. As Camilla stared at the bushes, a tiny head popped out and squeaked. Camilla sat there, rooted to the spot.

"Hello there. Aw, you're so cute. Come here, little guy," she said, smiling. The chipmunk sniffed, then scooted over right by her leg. "Wow, it's as if you have been around people before." The little chipmunk nodded his head.

"Whoa," Camilla breathed, "Can you understand me?" He nodded his small head again. Camilla stared at him in astonishment. Then she said, "This place is *full* of surprises." She picked him up.

Camilla heard a scuffling noise, and the little chipmunk scurried out of her hand and hid in the folds of her dress. Then Tracker appeared in the cave entrance with a plate of something brown and lumpy.

"Here."

"Ew, what in the world is that?"

Tracker's eyes narrowed. "Thissss isss your food. I'd eat it if I were you. Thisss isss the only meal you get during the day."

Camilla took the plate from him with a grim face. She muttered a brief thanks. Tracker turned and left the cave.

The little chipmunk reappeared from the folds of Camilla's dress. She poked at the unappetizing lump of what Tracker called "food." She sighed deeply.

"Well, little guy, are you hungry?" The chipmunk squeaked loudly. Camilla laughed at him as he tore into the goopy mess. She stuck her finger into the brown goo and into her mouth. Camilla swallowed grudgingly, making a disgusted face.

"Well, it isn't the best, but it'll have to do, Squeaker. I guess you're my only friend now," Camilla said as her hand patted Squeaker's goop-covered head.

CHAPTER 11

A Brief Reunion

"Oh, I can't believe she got captured. I was there, and I should have run after her. We *all* should have gone after her. What are we doing here? We need to be going after Camilla!" Ebeny said. She and Barron were walking with Shamoola, Ga, Sorin, and Poot down a long hall lined with portraits.

"You know why, Ebeny. It's dark out, and we have no plan or idea of where they are headed or what to do," Barron explained.

"Your father's right, Ebeny," King Shamoola said. "If we would have rushed blindly into the night and gotten lost, we'd have done Camilla no good." Sorin landed on the king's shoulder and nodded.

Ebeny knew what they were saying was true, but it was still frustrating. *Camilla, I wish you were here!* Ebeny thought.

Suddenly, a big gust of wind came and lifted her up into the air. As she was rising off the ground, she looked down and saw her body lying on the ground in a crumpled heap. She then realized that her soul was going on a journey that her body couldn't take. She stared in amazement as the vision of her unconscious self started to blur and then became obscured by a bright, white light. She couldn't see anything for what felt like only a few seconds. As the white light faded, a new picture came into view. Ebeny found herself sitting in a damp cave. Turning her head slightly to look behind her, she saw the night sky. Around the cave were at least a dozen campfires that illuminated the faces of gallops and creatures that looked to be a mixture of a snake and a crab. Turning back to look at the rest of the cave, Ebeny stared at the girl in front of her. The girl looked familiar to Ebeny. Confused, Ebeny gazed at the long, chestnut colored hair, the sad green eyes, the red gown she had worn to the feast. Ebeny couldn't believe her eyes. "Camilla!" Ebeny had landed right in front of her sister. She hadn't the faintest idea how it had happened, but she felt so glad to see her.

"Ebeny?" Camilla asked, turning her head in Ebeny's direction. Then her face lit up. She jumped up from the pile of scorched sticks that had a ring of charred stones circling it. "Ebeny, is it really you?" Camilla reached out to touch her sister, but her hand went straight through Ebeny's shimmering form.

"Yes, it's me. We're so worried about you. Are you all right?"

"I've been better, but at least I'm still alive. But what about you? You know you're translucent, right? I don't understand. What's happening? Are you a ghost?"

"I don't really understand it either. One minute I was in the castle, and I just started thinking about how much I wanted to see you. The next thing I knew, I was being whisked off here to you."

"I'm so glad to see you! Even if you do look like a ghost!" The sisters laughed, but quickly stopped when they heard a noise outside. After a few moments, when she was sure it was safe, Ebeny began speaking again.

"What's that?" Ebeny had just noticed the little brown ball of fur sitting at Camilla's feet.

"Oh, this is Squeaker. I found him in some bushes. I think he actually understands what we're saying."

"Squeak!"

"I see what you mean!" Ebeny giggled. "Where are you? We're going to rescue you."

"I don't know where I am. Some cave in the middle of the forest," Camilla replied.

"Well, try to stay safe. We'll find you. Don't—" Ebeny gasped, "What's happening to me?!" She was turning into dust, and floating up into the air.

Camilla stared at her with a horrified expression before crying, "No, wait! Come back!" Ebeny tried to stop herself from floating away, but failed. She stared sadly back at Camilla and waved.

Suddenly Camilla was gone and Ebeny was in the Enchanted Castle again. Shamoola, Ga, and her father were looking down at her with puzzled expressions. Sorin was there, too. *Ohhh boy, what happened?* Ebeny thought, looking around wildly.

"Ebeny! Ebeny, are you okay? You just collapsed on the floor." Barron was so happy his daughter was all right.

"I guess I'm okay, but I'm not really sure what just happened. I started thinking about how much I wanted to see Camilla, and then somehow I traveled to where she was. I mean not really traveled, but it was like my soul left my body and was transported to where the gallops were keeping Camilla captive."

Barron looked solemnly at Ga and King Shamoola.

King Shamoola's eyes smiled as he looked at Ebeny and stated, "It's time. You are ready to start."

"Start? Start what?" Ebeny looked to Barron for an explanation.

"Ebeny, there's something you need to understand. You and your sister are very special in many ways. That's why I brought you here. King Shamoola can help us discover and develop your abilities," Barron stated.

"Ebeny, please come with me now, before anything else causes any more delays. Come, take my hand for we are going someplace...different," King Shamoola coaxed. Then he turned to Barron and suggested, "Barron, please take Sorin and Ga and prepare for our rescue mission."

Barron nodded and put a reassuring hand on Ebeny's shoulder. She looked into his eyes and nodded curtly. "Come," Barron told Sorin and Ga. He began back the hall with the runkey and becon close behind.

Shamoola looked back to Ebeny and offered his arm. Ebeny looped her arm in his and walked down the hallway.

"Ebeny, what exactly happened back there? You said you had seen your sister. Can you explain it to me?" Shamoola asked as they continued walking.

Ebeny nodded and explained in a detailed description of her visit with Camilla. She also confessed her confusion of how she was able to travel that far without her body and why it had happened. Turning left, they continued down a second hallway.

Shamoola nodded. "It is called Spirit Gliding. Where a soul wants something desperately and separates from its body to get it. In this instant, you wished to see your sister, correct?"

"Yes," Ebeny replied faintly. She was amazed that it was even possible.

The king nodded again. "So your soul separated and flew to wherever your sister was."

Ebeny was still puzzled. "But how did my soul know where to go?"

Shamoola shrugged. "Even the smartest people in Zeoch together can't figure out how love works."

Ebeny nodded. It didn't make much sense, but she understood. She turned her concentration back to where she was going. At the end of the hallway, stairs appeared in front of her. They were rainbow colored, but also transparent. As she took her first step onto them, she fell through. Her eyes wandered to Shamoola and he nodded. It was as if he could read her mind. Ebeny tried again. This time when her foot sank down to the ground she kept going and put her other foot on the next step. *Wow! It didn't sink through!*

So Ebeny walked up farther and farther until she reached the top. Before her was a wide oak door. She heard a sound and turned to look. King Shamoola was right behind her.

"Go on, Ebeny, open the door." He sounded urgent, so with a huge shove, she swung the old oak door open. Ebeny felt a slight nudge and was pushed inside.

She looked around the dim room. At first all she saw was cobwebs, but as her eyes adjusted to the darkness, blobs took on definite shapes. One thing in particular that caught her eye was the table where King Shamoola was standing. It had a glowing crystal ball hovering over the green cloth that was on a table. He motioned for Ebeny to come to him.

As she slowly stepped over to him, a picture formed inside the ball. A hand, slow and steady, carefully lifted the lid of a glowing wooden box. The box had intricate designs etched in the surface, and Ebeny recognized it immediately. It was the box with the glowing letters that she and Camilla had seen in their room. Inside the box was something shimmering blue, but before Ebeny could see clearly what it was, the picture clouded over and disappeared.

Ebeny looked at Shamoola and said, "I just saw the box in our room."

"Look again."

Ebeny's eyes darted back to the crystal ball. A bronze key hovered in the mist inside. "A key," she murmured.

Shamoola urged, "Reach in and take it."

"What?"

"Reach in and take it," he repeated calmly.

Ebeny tentatively reached toward the crystal ball. Surprisingly, her fingers slipped right through the surface. Her fingers instantly felt cold. She stretched her hand farther into the mist and grasped the key, which felt even colder than the mist surrounding it. She stared, astounded, at the key for a few seconds before slowly pulling it out.

"Okay, this is a little too much," Ebeny said. Shamoola reached out and placed a calming hand on her arm.

"It's all right. I know that you have had some incredible experiences in a little amount of time. But if you want to save your sister, then we have no time to waste."

They walked down the rainbow stairs together. Ebeny looked out a window to her left and noticed that it was night-time. The moon shone brightly in the sky. On her way, a little star caught her eye, and she made a wish and knew Camilla would be all right.

Chapter 12

A Treasure in a Box

Ebeny's eyes scanned the glowing lettering on the box that was in her room. She reread it once more. It said, 'To open this box, you must find the key. Peer into the crystal, and you will see.' Now it all made sense to Ebeny. She had looked into the crystal, and she had seen the key. All she had to do was open the box.

A knock on the door startled her. Quickly recovering, Ebeny called out, "Come in." The door opened and Barron stepped casually in.

"Hello, my dear Ebeny. I just stopped in to check on you." Barron walked over to Ebeny. He held his arms out wide and gave his daughter a big hug.

Ebeny lightly pushed herself away from Barron and asked, "Are we ready to leave?"

"No, not quite. Shamoola and I still think that it would be wise to wait for daylight, but I promise we will leave with the sun's first rays."

Ebeny sighed and asked, "Won't the gallops be too far ahead if we don't leave right away?"

"We doubt that Camilla's captors will continue to travel in the dead of night."

"You are going to come in and get me before you leave, right?" Ebeny asked her father.

"Of course, but try to get a little sleep before then. You might also want to pack a few things for Camilla to change into since she is still in her dress and maybe a few other things, too. I have no idea how long we will be away from the castle. I just hope however long we are away, it will be with Camilla safe with us," Barron advised.

"Okay, thanks," Ebeny said.

Barron nodded. "Ebeny, tell me what happened with Shamoola."

Ebeny's eyes widened. She was unsure if she wanted to show Barron the key but supposed it was unavoidable. Standing up, she walked over to Barron and opened her hand. She offered him the key and he slowly took it. "Shamoola took me to a special room at the top of some magical rainbow steps. There was a table in the middle of the room with a crystal ball on it." Ebeny pointed to the glowing box in her room. "I saw that box in the crystal ball. Then a bronze key appeared, and

Shamoola told me to take it, so I reached in and pulled it out. I was just about to unlock the box when you came in," Ebeny finished. She looked into Barron's face and saw, to her surprise, understanding. Barron pressed the key lightly into the palm of Ebeny's hand.

He nodded and said, "I'll leave you to open it then. I'm sure you'll like what's inside. Good night." Barron smiled and walked out the door.

Ebeny was stunned. *How can he know what's in this box? Is the box his?* Shaking her head to clear away the thoughts, she walked back over to the box with the key tightly clenched in her hand.

Ebeny paused just in front of the box. She wondered what could've been so special to have been locked up like this. Looking down, Ebeny saw that the key was now throwing off a faint red glow just like the box. Her hand instinctively tightened its grip on the key. Ebeny moved her arm forward. She slowly slid the key into place and turned it. With a soft, *click,* the lid opened just a crack.

Ebeny stepped back, and then walked toward the box again. This time her hand, slow and steady, reached out and lifted the lid. The inside of the box was glowing. It was a red light and was too bright for Ebeny's eyes. She held her hand over her eyes as a shield. Then, suddenly, the box's bright light dimmed, and Ebeny removed her hand from her face. She could easily make out what was inside. Lying on a cushion of scarlet velvet was a shining sapphire butterfly. The wings were curved and covered in diamonds and sapphires. The body was made of sparkling silver. On the tips of the antennae were twinkling emeralds. Ebeny took her trembling hand off the lid and reached for the butterfly. Taking hold of it, she pulled upward and discovered that the enchanting butterfly was a necklace. The butterfly was connected to a silver chain.

Straightening her back, Ebeny slid the necklace over her head. She was about to shut the box when something else caught her eye. On the inside of the lid was a pocket that was hardly visible. Ebeny cautiously slid her hand into the pocket. Pulling out an old envelope, she saw, much to her surprise, that it had Camilla and Ebeny scribbled in fancy writing on the front of the card.

Ebeny stumbled clumsily over to a chair and sat down. As she tore open the envelope, a folded letter and two rings fell out. The rings reminded her of Barron's ring that helped him travel through the space slips. As she examined the rings more closely, she discovered that each ring had a name engraved on the inside. One read Ebeny, the other Camilla. She slipped the ring with her name on it on her right hand. Looking back at the letter, Ebeny unfolded it and began reading.

> My two dearest daughters,
>
> You must know that I love you more than anything. If you are reading this, then something must have happened to me. I planned to tell you myself when you were old enough, but I wrote this letter just in case something prevented my doing so.
>
> In this box, I have placed a few special items for you both. I wish for Ebeny to have my butterfly necklace. It will help channel your power.

Ebeny paused and looked at her mother's necklace dangling from her own neck. She looked back at the letter and continued to read.

To Camilla I am entrusting my pet. She is a small, deformed chog, but she will lay her life on the line for you. Her name is Ingline; treat her well. I told her to go to the Secret Valley of the Elves if anything went wrong. Hopefully, you will find her there still. I have also left two rings—one for each of you. They will allow you to go through the slips in space.

I trust that my good friend Shamoola and your wonderful father will watch you and make sure that you are safe. They will help you with any problem you may have.

Just remember that I love you.

Your Adoring Mother,

Ariona

Ebeny was stunned. She lightly stroked the necklace that once belonged to her mother. Without taking her eyes off her mother's letter, Ebeny stood up and walked over to her windowsill to sit down. *My mom must've sat in this same exact spot when she was living here,* Ebeny thought to herself in awe. Ebeny wished that Camilla were here now so that she could share this discovery with her.

"Wow, this is a letter from my mom," Ebeny mumbled quietly. Looking down, she reread one of the only connections she had to her mom.

Ebeny leaned back on the wall behind her. Closing her eyes, she tried to picture the mother she had lost. A few minutes later, Ebeny became tired. Sitting up, she went over to her mall-like closet and thought, *These clothes must have been my mother's when she was here.* Ebeny looked around for two pairs of jeans and two t-shirts. She found them at the back of the closet and put them into a drawstring bag she spotted on a shelf. Ebeny picked out another pair of jeans and a shirt and laid them out on her bed. After she quickly undressed, Ebeny put on the clean clothes and pulled her hair back. She set the bag of clothes on the floor by her bed.

Ebeny figured she should get a few hours of sleep. She gently pulled back the covers on her bed to reveal red satin sheets. She slid into her bed and slowly pulled the covers up to her chin. Her eyes closed and she started humming. Ebeny was again trying to put together a picture of what her mother would look like now. Just as she fell into a deep, dreamless sleep, Ebeny got a perfect picture of her mother holding two tiny babies in her arms—Ebeny and Camilla.

CHAPTER 13

A Light in the Dark

"**S**queak, squeak, squeak!"

"Squeaker, be quiet before we get in trouble!" Camilla said in a hoarse whisper to the little chipmunk beside her.

It appeared to be about midnight, for all the stars were out, and the moon was bright. Camilla gazed at them and wondered if Ebeny was looking at those very same stars. She thought about how Ebeny had just shown up earlier. She still didn't know how her sister had done it.

What did Ebeny tell me she did? I got it! All I must do is wish *to see Ebeny and I can* see Ebeny. *Simple, easy, and I'm going to try right now.* Camilla clasped her hands together and wished with all her might to see Ebeny and her body started to dissolve, like her soul, traveling to her sister. Suddenly, a bright white light obscured Camilla's vision. As quickly as the light appeared, it vanished. The next thing she knew, she was surrounded by darkness. Slowly, as her eyes adjusted, Camilla could make out shapes around her. She realized that she was standing in a big room. Camilla scanned the room about her. Sighing with relief, she realized that she was standing in the middle of her room in the Enchanted Castle. Looking for her sister, Camilla began to call out softly to her.

"Ebeny," Camilla whispered into the darkness. "Ebeny, where are you?"

From behind Camilla there was a loud groan and a confused reply. "Camilla, is that you?" Camilla could hear the hope in her sister's voice.

"Yeah, it's me Ebeny," Camilla confirmed with a smile. "I remembered you telling me how you came to my cave. I needed to see you again." Camilla paused and turned in a complete circle. "Where are you anyway? It's hard to see in the dark."

"Camilla, I'm right behind you. Turn around."

Behind her, Camilla heard a loud *THUD*. She turned to see an outline of a body stretched out on the floor.

"What was that? Ebeny, are you okay?"

"Yeah, I'm fine. The rug tripped me."

"You've got to watch out for those rugs. They're dangerous," Camilla warned with a smile on her lips. Ebeny laughed softly and stood up. Walking over to a table, Ebeny leaned forward and laid her hand gently on what appeared to be a lamp. Gradually a bright yellow light filled the room and illuminated everything. Camilla blinked in the sudden brightness.

"What is that?" Camilla asked in awe. "I didn't think this world had electricity."

Ebeny shook her head. "They don't," she replied. "Shamoola explained that it's a magical energy borrowed from the living things around it."

Camilla was horrified. "You mean it's eating our energy?"

"Well, yeah, I suppose. I was freaked out, too. But Shamoola told me that the lamps use such a small amount of energy that you never notice it."

"That's okay, then," Camilla relented.

Ebeny walked back over to Camilla. After staring at Camilla's form for a while, Ebeny commented, "You look like a ghost."

"So did you when you came to me," Camilla countered.

Ebeny shrugged, a simple shift in the shadows of the room. "Well, I guess that's what happens when you spirit glide."

"Is that what this is called? Spirit gliding?"

"Yeah, Shamoola told me, along with some other things. You know that glowing box we found earlier?"

Camilla nodded, "Yes. What about it?"

"Well, it contained some of our mother's things. Like this." Ebeny reached into her shirt and lifted out the sapphire butterfly necklace so Camilla could see it more clearly.

"It's beautiful!" Camilla gasped. She reached out and lightly ran her finger along the edge of the butterfly. As she removed her finger, Ebeny tucked the necklace back inside her shirt.

"There were also two rings that look like Barron's. They have our names engraved on the inside of each ring." Ebeny walked over to the table beside her bed and picked up the ring with Camilla's name on it. "Here." She held it out for Camilla.

Camilla reached out, but her hand passed right through Ebeny's, leaving the ring untouched. "Dang it! I guess I can't touch anything when I'm in spirit form. Keep it safe for me. Give it to me when you rescue me. You are planning to rescue me, right?"

"Of course we are! Dad and I were ready to leave right after the gallops took you, but Shamoola convinced us that it would be better to wait for daylight with a plan in place instead of rushing blindly out into the night."

Camilla sighed, "I understand, but hurry! We're going to move again in the morning. I miss you already."

Ebeny noticed Camilla's fingers beginning to disappear. "Camilla, you're dissolving into air!."

Camilla gasped and looked at her disappearing body. "I can feel it. Goodbye, Ebeny!"

"Goodbye, Camilla! We'll rescue you soon. I promise!" Ebeny watched as her sister's translucent form dissolved completely, and Ebeny was alone once again.

Oh, good, it is my special cave in which I, Camilla Goldenheart Swallowtail, live! she thought, sarcastically. As Camilla was floating down, a squeak told her that a little friend had been waiting for her. She found on the floor an almost empty plate of the brown goo that Tracker had said was "food." She bent down to sniff the cold brown stuff. It smelled horrid; the very stench filled her nose and caused her to gag.

Camilla sighed and said, "Yuck, I'm glad at least *someone* likes this slop. I know I don't," Camilla paused for a moment as her loud voice echoed through the cave. "I think we should go to sleep now," she said with an almost hoarse whisper.

As she walked toward the back of the cave, the frost-covered leaves cracked under her scratched, filthy, party shoes. Her dress got caught in a few small, spiky brambles that were growing from a crack in the cave wall.

"Ugh. I'm not in the mood for you tonight, Mr. Bush-on-wall. Hey, what's this? That's a pretty rock." A smooth, purple stone tumbled out of the brambles and landed in the leaves in front of her.

She picked it up and found that it was quite warm even though it had probably been there for a while. Camilla looked at Squeaker and carried the warm stone over to her bed of moss and leaves that she had made earlier that evening.

"Scoot over, little guy. I need room, too. Goodnight, my friend." She said a silent prayer and went to sleep.

Sometime in the night, Camilla had a dream that Ga, her father, Ebeny, Sorin, King Shamoola, and Poot rescued her. Then a smile crossed her face, and she fell into a deeper sleep. And somehow, a light seemed to glow from her, a soft light in the dark.

CHAPTER 14

Time to Save Camilla

C a zoomed just inside the open door of King Shamoola's bedroom. A mechanical hand shot out of the bottom of his body and knocked on the door frame. Shamoola turned to look in Ga's direction. Without moving from his position at the window, Shamoola said, "Come in, Ga." The becon went over to hover beside Shamoola.

"Are we ready to leave, yet?" Shamoola asked, still gazing out the window at the night sky. Ga noticed that the sky was growing faintly lighter in the far off distance.

"It's nearly sunrise. We are all ready, but the rest of our group is still sleeping. We will have to wake them soon," Ga informed him.

Shamoola nodded. "Yes. Ga, get the group together and ready in the courtyard. I will gather our supplies and talk to my steward and let him know what to do in my absence. Once we are all ready, we will depart with the first rays of sun at our backs."

"Excellent. Let's get the rest of our group," Ga suggested.

"Of course. I'll follow you." Shamoola motioned to Ga and followed him out the door.

Sitting on the window seat in her room, Ebeny sighed. "I hope my wish comes true—my wish to save Camilla." She got up from her seat on the windowsill, walked over to her bed, sat down, and started crying into her rose-colored pillow. She sniffed then thought, *I should try singing. It always used to make me feel better. How did that one song go that my dad taught me? Oh, yes.* Ebeny took a breath, and then started.

> *"Close your eyes and you will see*
> *That you are not alone.*
> *Search your heart and you will find*
> *The truth you've always known.*

"Oh what's the use! Singing will never help me feel better. Oh Camilla, I miss you!" Ebeny started crying again, but she quickly regained control of her sorrow. "Okay, Ebeny, calm down. Let's try this again.

> *"There is magic within you*
> *Just waiting to bloom.*
> *There's a fire in your soul.*
> *Ignite it and soon*
> *You'll see what you can be*
> *If only you believe."*

She stopped and walked over to sit at the window again, but she didn't know that Barron was standing right outside the door.

When he heard her singing, Barron froze with his hand on the door knob and stared at the door. Ariona used to sing that song to help Ebeny and Camilla fall asleep. Ariona had eventually taught the song to Barron who taught his daughters.

As soon as Ebeny sat down, she felt the tiniest bit of hope flicker up inside her heart. In a low voice she began once again.

> *"Close your eyes and you will see*
> *That you are not alone.*
> *Search your heart and you will find*
> *The truth you've always known."*

At that moment, Barron turned the door knob and knocked gently on the door. Ebeny's head whipped around and looked with surprise at her father's face peering around the door. "Ebeny? May I come in?" he asked.

Ebeny nodded, wondering if he heard her singing.

Barron walked over and stood beside her. "That was beautiful."

Ebeny blushed slightly and began twisting her hair around her finger. She didn't like it when other people heard her singing.

"It's time to go. Are you sure you wish to accompany us?"

"Of course. Why wouldn't I?"

"It's going to be very dangerous, you know."

Ebeny nodded, "I know. But she's my sister, and I promised her that I'd rescue her."

Barron smiled proudly, "I thought you'd say that. We need to get moving. Gather what you've packed. We need to meet Shamoola in the courtyard." Barron leaned down and kissed Ebeny on the head. "Don't worry. We'll find her."

Ebeny stood up and retrieved the drawstring bag from the side of her bed. Slinging it over her shoulder, she followed Barron out of the room. At the doorway, she turned and looked back at her mother's box. Making a silent promise to Ariona that they would save Camilla, Ebeny turned and walked briskly after her father.

Chapter 15

A New Location

Crack... the charcoal broke again.

Camilla sighed. She was trying to draw a picture of Squeaker on the cave wall, but it looked more like a bush with a tail than a chipmunk. Camilla's captors had begun traveling before the sun was up and stopped near a stream around the beginning of afternoon. She was sent to a cave similar to the one she had left. Even though the cave wall was smooth, Camilla still couldn't control the small piece of charred wood she had picked out from the old fire pit that had been there when Camilla arrived. She presumed it was from travelers who had stopped there before her. Camilla lay back on the cool cave floor. She closed her eyes and thought back to before Blackess had come. She remembered her school and the library. She thought about events on Earth that would be coming up shortly. *It's too bad I'll be missing Easter. It's about a month away, I think.*

"You know what, Squeaker? It should be my birthday soon. I'll be thirteen on March 5." Squeaker squeaked in response. "I wonder if Ebeny and Dad will remember even if we are in Zeoch." Camilla laughed. Camilla was about to speak again when she felt something shaking in her pockets. She reached into her pocket, pulled out the purple stone, and set it on the ground in front of her. She knelt down by the stone and watched it shake. *What's going on here? Why is it shaking?. Hold up, what's that?* A few small cracks stretched across the smooth surface.

Squeaker scrambled up onto Camilla's lap and leaned against her stomach. The stone shook much more fiercely. Suddenly it broke open. Tiny pieces of the stone fell on the cave floor. A small, slimy, scaly thing rolled out.

It was about the size of a newborn kitten and the color of an eggplant. It had four small wings that looked leathery and were folded up against its slick body. Its eyes were a stormy gray. The head was diamond-shaped with small spikes sticking out of the top of its head. Underneath its chin, small bumps stood out. As Camilla's eyes passed over the tail, she noticed that it was long, but muscular. The tail ended gradually in a sharp point. A thought passed through her head, *What is this strange creature?*

"Hey, little girl." Camilla jumped when the four-winged thing lifted its head and nodded in hello. "Wow. You understand me, too?" The tiny creature nodded again. "Incredible. This world is full of amazing animals. You look like a miniature dragon."

Squeaker jumped off Camilla's lap and scampered over to it. Camilla reached out slowly with her fingers extended. She tried to touch the four-winged dragon. It flinched away then nudged back and rubbed its head lightly against her fingertips. The horns on its head were somewhat sharp, but they didn't puncture Camilla's skin.

Her fingers tingled where the creature had touched her. She stared in wonder at the small dragon and pulled her hand slowly back. She heard the sound of gallops trotting her way. Camilla grabbed the tiny dragon and Squeaker. She hid them in the pockets of her dress. She had thought it odd that such a fancy dress had pockets, but she was certainly glad she had them now.

"Please, stay quiet, please," Camilla begged them. She straightened up and faced the cave entrance.

Suddenly, two eyes appeared around the side of the cave. The gallop's eyes scanned the area, and then he brought out the rest of his body before speaking. «We're moving. Some of us believe that we are being tracked. Brashong will be in charge of you.» He paused to motion at a gallop behind him.

Brashong was a much smaller gallop than the rest. He tripped as he walked up to meet her. The color was different, too. Instead of a bright olive, Brashong had a dark green upper body and white lower body. The other gallop turned and left.

«Hi.»

"Um—hi to you, too." Camilla paused; then, without thinking, she blurted out, "Why are you a different color than the rest of the gallops?" As soon as the words were out of her mouth, she regretted saying them. She expected him to be really mad at her and to vaporize her with his eyes. Instead, he simply nodded as if he had gone through this before.

«Well, my father, Brenas, was this color, too. Darker gallops like us are pretty rare I guess. Personally, I like this color better.» This gallop was friendly, she wasn't sure why he was in a group as mean as this.

Camilla was shocked. "Your father was Brenas?"

Brashong nodded and smiled. «I was young when he died in the war, so I don't remember him very well.»

Camilla smiled. "Someone I know does. Do you have a brother?" she asked.

«Yes. He is older than I am. His name is Poot,» Brashong explained.

"Yeah, he's my friend. He sort of saved us from a pack of gallops when we first came into Zeoch."

Brashong eyed her suspiciously. «When and where did you first enter Zeoch?»

Camilla thought for a second. "I'm not sure when exactly. My sister Ebeny and I came from Earth."

Brashong's eyes widened. «You are one of The Last Two! Some of the other gallops had doubts, but none were sure. Amazing,» Brashong exclaimed, looking at Camilla with a new respect. All of a sudden, there was a short little "hrrrrk" from the pocket of her dress. Camilla and Brashong both looked down as the little dragon poked its head out of her pocket . It turned its scaly head and stared up at them.

Brashong looked at Camilla questioningly. "Don't tell the other gallops," Camilla told him. He nodded at her, and she smiled back.

"Okay, Brashong, I found this stone in the back of the cave I was in last night. I picked it up, and felt that it was warm. So I kept it. Then, a few minutes ago, it cracked open and this came out," She explained quickly.

«That little animal that came out of the stone, she is a presipatice, a small form of dragon.» He seemed to be a little surprised himself at this candor.

Camilla, grateful to have someone speaking kindly to her, said, "You know, I consider your brother one of my friends. I suppose that makes you my friend, too."

«Being friends with a prisoner is unacceptable.» Camilla's smile faded. «But I feel like I could make an exception in your case, as long as it's our secret.»

Camilla's smile reappeared. "Deal," she said. A sudden thought crossed her mind as she reached out to shake his hand, *Wow, this is perfect, a friend inside my enemies.*

«Well then, let's get a move on. General Shale would like to start moving as soon as possible,» Brashong said calmly and walked out of the cave. Camilla slipped her hand in her pocket to keep the little dragon from showing her head again. The little dragon hummed contentedly.

When Camilla and Brashong exited the cave, they saw that all the creatures were standing in a group ready to go. The group parted to let Camilla and Brashong pass. Some of them purposely bumped Camilla and made cruel remarks. Camilla gave all of the creatures who taunted her murderous looks, but that only made them laugh harder. When they made it to Shale, he looked deeply disturbed.

«My elf prisoner, Camilla, how nice of you to join us.» He paused. A few hushed snickers passed through the crowd. Shale gave them a look that said, "Stop laughing now or you'll all die." Camilla could hardly suppress a smirk of satisfaction. «I just received a mynapathy message from a gallop in Gorgon's castle. He says that we need to move quickly so there is no risk of anyone catching up to us.» Shale seemed to be waiting for Camilla to say something. Instead she just stood there.

«You will be escorted by Brashong and Tracker, and you will most likely have to run in order to keep up,» Shale said as the big bambargle strode up to her. Shale continued, «They will tie a rope around you so you do not run away or even think about running away.» He then nodded to Tracker who wrapped a thick piece of rope firmly around Camilla's middle. She didn't protest, but she certainly didn't like it. Tracker tied the other end of the rope around his claw. Camilla's face looked angry, but she controlled her emotions well.

«Now,» Shale was addressing all the other creatures, «Form your marching position and *march*.» All of the gallops and bambargles moved into a tight oval around Camilla, Brashong, and Tracker. They all moved forward quickly. Camilla's hopes of being rescued plummeted. She knew that it was nearly impossible for Barron and the others to rescue her now; they had to catch a moving target.

Camilla ran as fast as she could, but soon was exhausted. She tried to slow down, but Tracker yanked on the rope to make her go faster. Although Tracker kept pulling on the rope, Camilla's legs refused to move any faster than they were already going. The creatures behind her were groaning and getting annoyed. Their general was ahead of them, and they were stuck behind a lowly prisoner.

"Prisssoner," Tracker said. His tone was annoyed and worried.

"My name isn't prisoner; it's Camilla," Camilla snapped. Brashong shot her a warning glance, but Camilla ignored it. Tracker glared at Camilla.

"That may be, but I prefffer to call you prisssoner. Move fassster." Tracker then yanked the rope and tore ahead. Camilla had to struggle to keep up.

«Are you okay?» Brashong spoke only to Camilla. She nodded slightly without even looking at him. She knew he would probably be punished for showing such kindness.

It was evening when General Shale finally called a halt. They had stopped in the middle of a clearing by a fast-flowing stream. The trees were thick and surrounded the clearing except for the gap that they had come through. Behind that was a small range of hills and miles and miles of endless forest. To Camilla's right was a large boulder that had a huge hole in its side. Tracker leaned over and snipped at the rope that squeezed her stomach. Camilla continued to breathe heavily from running nonstop and was glad the suffocating rope was gone.

"Sssit in that clussster of bouldersss over there. I will then bring you fffood." To Brashong, Tracker ordered, "Stay close to the elf and watch her." Brashong nodded and turned his eyes to Camilla. She nodded thankfully and limped off to the three big rocks with Brashong following behind. When both Camilla and Brashong were inside the boulders, Camilla collapsed against the cool rock wall. Brashong knelt down beside her.

«Do you want some water from the stream?» His eyes showed how worried he was. Camilla's face was slightly pale, and sweat drenched her filthy face. She said nothing but merely nodded. He stood up and galloped away. Squeaker and the miniature dragon peeked their heads out of the pockets of Camilla's dress. Camilla reached down and grabbed hold of the little chipmunk. The dragon slipped out of her pocket and curled up in Camilla's lap.

"Hello, Sparkle." The dragon looked at her, puzzled at her new name. With her free hand, she stroked Sparkle's head caringly. Just then Brashong rushed in with a small jug of water. He bent down to hand it to Camilla.

"Thanks, Brashong." She took hold of the jug before putting it to her lips and drinking the cold water greedily. When she finished, Camilla handed the jug back to Brashong, and he set it in the corner.

«Is there anything else I can do for you?» Brashong asked.

Camilla shrugged and looked around the boulders. There was nothing for her to sleep on. The water jug was now empty. She looked back at the expressionless face of Brashong and said, "Let's try to make this place a bit more comfortable. Would you be able to bring me some moss or something for a bed? Then, after that, can you get some more water? I'm a bit thirsty," Camilla smiled sheepishly.

Brashong nodded. «Okay. See you later.» And with that, Brashong quietly slipped into the surrounding forest.

CHAPTER 16

Gallop Camp

The glowing sun spilled across Ebeny's face as it lifted into the sky. The animals that were hiding in the brush and wood stirred and awakened. Ebeny's eyes blinked open and searched the area around her.

Bumps on the ground started looking like her friends. Ga was hovering nearby under a tree. Barron was sleeping by her side and Shamoola on the other side of Barron. Poot was kneeling in the shadows.

Only after Ebeny looked about her did she remember where she was. It was the second day of their travel. The area around her was damp and cold. Water dripped from all of the tall trees. *It must have rained. But why didn't I feel anything?* Ebeny tilted her head upward. She noticed that a thick covering of leaves acted like a roof over her head; obviously Barron had done it during the night. It was woven together carefully, like he did when they used to go on camping trips. Barron and Shamoola had a leaf roof as well.

She was startled by a rustling noise to her left. It was Sorin, waddling in that weird way of his out of the bushes, carrying some seeds and nuts. He dropped them by the fire pit and came over to sit by her.

"When do you think Barron and Shamoola will wake up?" Ebeny asked Sorin casually. To her left, the little runkey shrugged in response.

Behind the two of them, a deep voice said loudly, "How about right now?" Ebeny and Sorin twisted around to stare at the tall, muscular man. "Are you ready to go, Ebeny?" Barron asked.

"Of course," Ebeny said as she leapt up.

"So am I," Shamoola announced from beside Barron, with Poot by his side.

"Great! Let's go," Barron ordered.

As soon as they started to move again, Sorin took off into the sky. He was the group's lookout. Poot dropped behind to watch if they were being followed.

After an hour of walking, Barron slowed and turned to Ebeny. He asked, "How would you like to learn some magic today?"

"Seriously?"

Barron nodded.

"Definitely," Ebeny said excitedly as she slowed, too.

Barron called up to Sorin, "Mr. Runkey, do come down here!" With a slight twist of his wings, Sorin made a nose-dive and landed easily on Ebeny's shoulder. Barron continued, "Shamoola tells me you have experience with teaching elves. We hope to catch up to the gallops soon, and I'd like Ebeny to be ready for anything we encounter. Do you know any useful attacking spells?"

"Actually, I do," Sorin responded proudly. "All you have to do, Ebeny, is say rashu, and the thing that you point at will explode into a huge blaze. If you only want a small flame, just think small. You have to envision what you want to happen, see it in your mind. Once you see the fire, say rashu and whatever you saw in your head will become reality. Go ahead now; try it."

The group halted for Ebeny to try out the spell. "Okay, rashu!" The tree in front of Ebeny sparked into a small flame. After a few seconds the flame went out and left smoke hanging in the air. "Let's try this again," Ebeny said. "Rashu!" Her voice was strong. Ariona's necklace felt warm against her chest. Ebeny's hands flew forward, and a blinding light erupted from them. Sorin was thrown backward from the jerking motion Ebeny had made. He ended up sitting in a bush while Ebeny stood firmly in place. The light lasted no more than five seconds. The tree Ebeny had directed the spell at was now mainly ashes. When Ebeny's hands came back to her sides, Sorin clamored back onto her shoulder and said, "Great. Next time, warn me before you do a spell." Ebeny blushed and smiled sheepishly, while everyone around her burst into astounded laughter.

"Well done, Ebeny." Barron praised.

"You must be powerful if you turned a tree to ash before you were trained properly," Shamoola remarked.

"Thanks," Ebeny said.

"Sorin, scout ahead and report back as soon as you can," Barron ordered. The runkey nodded and shot into the sky. The group continued to walk quickly forward. After a short time, Sorin came back and landed on Barron's shoulder.

"There is a cluster of hills up ahead. Camilla's captors are camping there, but I doubt for much longer," Sorin reported.

"Thank you," Barron said and dismissed Sorin who flew into the sky just above the group's heads.

An hour later, the wandering group caught sight of a ridge of hills on the horizon. Barron and Shamoola called a halt to the weary and excited group.

"Sorin says that over those hills is the gallop camp and my daughter. Once we get to the top, we'll have to stay low and keep quiet—except you, Ebeny. You are to stay here. I don't want anything to happen to you. Sorin will stay with you." Sorin looked just as surprised as Ebeny.

"What!? Why can't I come? I mean, you just taught me rashu, or was that just for entertainment?" Ebeny argued.

Barron sighed.

Shamoola explained, "Your father doesn't want anything to happen to you, and neither do I. We wanted to teach you rashu so you could defend yourself, but we don't want to put you in harm's way if there's anything we can do to stop it." Ebeny crossed her arms and held in a sharp response. Sorin mirrored her angry stance while sitting on Ebeny's shoulder. The elder men nodded; Barron's emerald eyes hinted a bit of sorrow, but Shamoola's dark violet eyes showed his hidden amusement at

Ebeny's and Sorin's actions. They led Poot and Ga onward. Sorin took off after them and was back in no time.

"Ebeny," he started, "I saw another path that leads up the hills. If we take that path, I don't think the others will see us. If we move as quick as a wark, I'm sure we could get to the hills in enough time, just in case they do need us."

Ebeny nodded and smiled, "I have no idea what a wark is, but let's go!" She gave the little runkey a hug and raced into the forest.

In about five minutes, Ebeny was at the top of one of the large hills and looking down on the gallop camp. She scanned the area and told the runkey to scout ahead. He nodded and took off. Ebeny carefully stepped down the hill. She had only gone a few yards when she sighted three gallops coming her way. Ebeny tried not to panic, but her breathing quickened and her fingers twisted in around her jet black hair.

"Ebeny!" Sorin whispered loudly into her ear. Ebeny jumped before looking at him angrily.

"What was that for!? You nearly gave me a heart attack!" she whispered harshly back at him. Sorin shrugged to answer her.

He turned to point at a cluster of boulders not too far away. He twisted his head back to say in a hoarse voice, "Over there is Camilla. I saw her in there and she looks extremely depressed." Ebeny nodded. She looked a bit happier, but her eyes still had deep fear in them. Sorin noticed this. "I'll go distract those bozos while you go grab Camilla."

"But shouldn't we wait for Dad?"

"I'm sure he'll be here any minute, but we have no time to lose. Don't worry; just run into the forest and I'll find you. Use the spell I taught you if there's any trouble."

Ebeny stared at him with wide eyes. "Sorin, you—" She tried to say something, but Sorin was already off, yelling insults at the gallops. Ebeny couldn't help smiling. She whipped around and sped off to Camilla's boulders.

She burst through the opening, rushed over to Camilla, and gave her a big hug before getting serious.

"Camilla! Hurry, we have to go. Sorin's distraction won't keep them at bay for long."

Camilla stared flabbergasted at her sister. Then heeding her advice, she jumped to her feet and gave Ebeny a quick hug while saying, "Boy, am I glad to see you! Let's go!" When she had collected her chipmunk and dragon, the two girls grabbed hands and dashed out of the entrance.

The elves managed to get halfway across the camp before a gallop noticed them. He leapt up and immediately started to chase the sisters.

Ebeny turned around, put up her hands and screamed "RASHU!" at their pursuers. There was a flash of red light, and the gallop turned to dust and ash.

Ebeny stumbled. Camilla looked astounded, but stopped and took her sister's arm, "Whoa. That was amazing! Are you okay?"

"I'm fine. That spell just took a lot out of me. Let's go. We have to get out of here."

They were almost to the woods before a group of gallops and bambargles thundered up behind them. Once again Ebeny turned around, raised her hands, and hollered with all her might "RASHU!!" A bambargle was destroyed this time The remaining bambargles and gallops stopped in their tracks in shock while Camilla and Ebeny escaped into the woods.

Ebeny collapsed in exhaustion at the base of a large rock. Camilla sat down beside her and asked, "Are you sure you're okay?"

"Yeah. Just give me a minute to rest. I didn't realize using that spell would make me so tired. I guess I have to be careful not to use it very often."

"How did you learn to do that?"

"Sorin taught me, along with encouragement from Dad and Shamoola."

"Ebeny, how did you get here so fast?"

"We came fast as possible. We only stopped once, and that was because we just couldn't keep our eyes open any longer!"

"So, where is Dad? And you said we, who else came?"

"Dad should be here with Ga, Poot, and Shamoola. They had me and Sorin stay behind, but we wanted to help so we ran as fast as we could to get here. We thought they would be here, but, I guess they aren't. I was just so worried about you, Camilla, that I couldn't wait for them," Ebeny explained.

"Wow, I have a really great family, and friends, too, although I would say that they *are* kind of my family. You and me, we're probably the luckiest half-elf sisters in the world." Ebeny smiled and nodded at her sister.

Then, suddenly, a dark green gallop burst out of the woods with Sorin on his back. «Hi. You must be Ebeny. I am...»

"A gallop! Camilla, this is a gallop, and it knows my name!"

"It's okay, Ebeny. I will explain. Don't worry, everything is just fine."

The Last Two were together once again.

CHAPTER 17

Finding What Was Lost

As Barron, Shamoola, Poot, and Ga were approaching the gallop camp, their eyes saw wisps of smoke curling into the bright, blue sky. They hesitated no more than a few seconds before dashing up the hill. A couple of smoldering heaps of ashes lay around the camp. The rest of the creatures were slightly dazed and stupefied. They hurriedly were gathering together in the middle of the camp and setting off into the forest.

"Ebeny. It had to have been Ebeny. But how could she have gotten here before us?" Barron observed out loud.

«She was determined to help,» Poot muttered.

"She mastered that spell very quickly," Shamoola said. The rest of them nodded. They slunk into the camp and went over to where the group of creatures had been standing.

"Look!" Ga shouted. A hand popped out from him to point at two pairs of footprints leading to the forest; one was slightly bigger than the other.

Barron walked over and kneeled beside the prints. He traced them with his finger. "These are definitely the girls' prints. Sorin must have been flying, so his prints won't be here." He got up and followed the trail to the surrounding forest. Ga, Shamoola, and Poot followed hesitantly.

After going a few feet into the woods, Ga paused. "Look at these prints."

Barron looked at the prints and frowned. "These are gallop prints with Ebeny's and Camilla's. We must hurry before something bad happens."

"Do you think we're far enough into this bramble thicket yet?" Ebeny asked.

"I don't think we could ever be far enough away from General Shale," Camilla remarked with a shiver.

«Yes. Let's keep moving a little farther and hope it's safe enough,» Brashong suggested.

"Okay," the sisters agreed. The little group moved deeper into the brambles.

"Ouch!" Camilla exclaimed. Sorin was startled and flapped into the air before quickly landing on Brashong's back again.

«I'm sorry. I didn't mean to step on your toe. My mind was somewhere else,» Brashong apologized.

"Where was it? Are you regretting helping us?" Ebeny questioned as she stepped over a bramble bush.

«Never! Helping you is the best decision I've made in quite a while. My mind was wandering back to the time before I was forced to join Gorgon's army,» Brashong hastily explained.

Ebeny looked confused. She slowed down to walk beside him and laid her hand on his arm. "What? You mean that you didn't want to be a part of Gorgon's army?" Brashong shook his head slowly. Camilla stepped in front of Brashong in order to lay a hand gently on his arm.

«I didn't and still don't, but my mother and the rest of the gallops forced me to stay.» The sisters smiled and patted his arms.

They began walking but stopped again when they heard a grumbling noise. Camilla held a hand on her stomach and blushed. Squeaker and Sparkle poked their heads out of the pockets to see what the noise was. "Sorry. I haven't really eaten since the feast." She noticed Sparkle and Squeaker and gently patted both their heads and pushed them back into her pockets.

"What were those?" Ebeny asked.

"They're my pets. Squeaker is a chipmunk and Sparkle is a tiny four winged dragon," Camilla explained.

"Whoa! I want to see them."

"Okay. Here." Camilla reached into her pockets and pulled out Sparkle and handed her to Ebeny. She put Squeaker on her hand for Ebeny to see.

"That's amazing," Ebeny whispered and handed Sparkle back to Camilla.

"I keep them in my pockets so they can stay safe," Camilla explained as she slid the squirming pets into her pockets.

Ebeny looked quizzically at Camilla's dress. "Your dress has pockets?"

"Yeah. They're really handy."

"Cool. Now about you being hungry," Ebeny began.

Brashong pointed at a bush behind Camilla. «There's a paffleberry bush. It's dark pink berries are quite delicious. You have to be careful when you pick berries; some of them are highly poisonous.»

"Thanks, Brashong." The older sister walked over to the bush covered in berries. She bent down, picked a large berry, and popped it into her mouth. "Mmm, Brashong, you were right. These really are delicious!" She leaned over and picked some more. Standing up again, Camilla groaned.

"Ugh. I really wish I hadn't worn this dress to the feast. It is so hard to move in and they made me run in this," she complained.

Ebeny grimaced. "Yeah, it must be uncomfortable, but you look pretty." Camilla smiled as Ebeny reached for the drawstring bag on her back and pulled it off her shoulders. She opened it and pulled out a pair of pants and a shirt. "Here, Dad had me bring these for you."

"Thank you, Dad. I'll change into them now," Camilla said as she took the clothes and moved deeper into the bushes to put them on. Ebeny knelt and continued to pick the paffleberries. When Camilla reemerged, she sat with her sister, Brashong, and Sorin and enjoyed the berries. Camilla slipped a few berries into both of her pockets for her pets to eat. She heard a faint chewing sound and was glad her pets enjoyed the berries.

A few moments later, the group had finished the berries and were about to continue on through the forest when they heard rustling in the woods behind them. The group jumped up. The rustling became steadily louder, and they saw bushes swish in front of them. Brashong stepped in front of the sisters as his eyes began to glow. Ebeny held out her hands, ready to use rashu. Camilla picked up a fallen branch and held it in front of her. Sorin picked up a few nuts, ready to throw them. Out of the bushes, stepped Barron, Ga, Poot, and Shamoola. The sisters and Sorin sighed in relief and dropped their weapons. Brashong noticed their behavior and his eyes returned to normal. The first thing Barron's group noticed was the small dark green and white gallop standing in front of Camilla and Ebeny with Sorin hovering over his back.

"Camilla, Ebeny, get away from that gallop now," Barron's voice was stern, "*Now.*" Barron held his hands out as sparks flew from his palms.

Camilla and Ebeny looked at Barron in fright. "Dad! No, don't hurt him; he's with us," Camilla shouted. She got up and went over to him. Barron bent down and hugged her. Ebeny went over to her father and he hugged her, too.

He pushed Camilla and Ebeny away from him and asked Camilla, "Are you all right?"

"Yeah," Camilla answered.

Barron smiled and turned to Ebeny. "You should have waited near the edge of the woods for us. I was very worried. We all were," he explained.

"Sorry. I wasn't thinking. I just wanted to get Camilla, Sorin, Brashong, and me away from the camp. I didn't want her to get captured again," Ebeny explained. Barron nodded his acceptance and turned to look inquiringly at Brashong.

"How'd you find us?" Camilla asked dumb-founded. "I thought we had a pretty good hiding place."

"This is a good hiding place," Shamoola answered. "But your trail was pretty obvious," he added with a laugh.

"We knew we couldn't wait around the gallop camp in case the creatures came after us, so we just kept moving," Ebeny added.

"They didn't look like they were going to come after you. They seemed to be in a state of confusion. As we snuck through the camp, they were starting to move out. Do you know what happened there?" Shamoola inquired.

"With the spell Sorin taught me, I know I destroyed a couple of the creatures, but certainly not all of them. They were all that confused that they left?" Ebeny asked.

"It seemed so. They were most likely going to get reinforcements and didn't want to come after a dangerous elf," Barron suggested. "So who is your young gallop friend?"

Brashong walked over to Ga and King Shamoola. «I am a gallop named Brashong, the son of Brenas, and brother to...» He never finished because at that moment, his eyes fell upon his brother Poot.

«Me.» Poot said. Shamoola, Barron, and Ga gaped at him. Suddenly Poot asked him, «Do you want to join our little group to protect these elves from Gorgon?» This time Brashong gaped at him. His eyes wandered to everyone's face.

«I w-would be most honored.» As he said this, he stood taller and puffed out his chest a little.

"I guess our little band is back together, now, but where in the world are we going to go that's safe enough?" The question hung over their heads, making the air around them tense. No one knew the answer to Shamoola's question, not quite yet.

CHAPTER 18

Preparing for the Unexpected

"Camilla, I'm so glad we saved you. If we hadn't, nobody would be here to entertain me," Ebeny said as she fed Squeaker and Sparkle.

"So that's all I am to you—entertainment?" Camilla asked with a grin.

"Stop it. You know what I mean."

"Yeah, I do. You mean that you're glad I found Squeaker and Sparkle for you to play with, and you didn't miss me at all," Camilla said in jest.

Squeaker squeaked and cocked his head as if he really believed the sisters were truly on the verge of an argument.

"Don't worry, Squeaker. Camilla can be the queen of sarcasm when she wants to be. But she knows how much she means to me. I don't know what I would've done if something bad had happened to her."

"Thanks, Ebeny. I love you, too," Camilla said.

Barron smiled at his daughters, relieved that they were reunited once again. For the last few hours, since everyone had been reunited, Barron, Shamoola, Ga, and Poot had been discussing what they should do next. Their goal was to get the girls to safety. Barron had liked Brashong's suggestion the best. He had said that they should take them to the Secret Valley of the Elves. It was safe, and although there were no elves left to take care of the gardens, food and water would still be plentiful there. The Valley also had secret caves to hide in and was protected by ancient elfin magic.

"How long will it take to get to the Secret Valley of the Elves?" Ebeny asked Barron.

"A few days, a week at the most," Barron replied as he tightened a pack of food onto Poot's back.

"That's not too long," Ebeny remarked.

Barron shook his head. "No, it shouldn't be, as long as we keep moving." He stepped away from Poot and over to Shamoola.

"Ready to go?" Barron asked. Shamoola tighten the ropes that held a few smaller bags filled with extra clothes, something soft to sleep on, and bottles for water.

"Now I am," Shamoola said. "Let's go."

«Do you want me in the back again?» Poot asked.

"Yes, thanks," Barron agreed.

«What do you want me to do?» Brashong asked, moving back beside his brother.

"Go back with your brother to watch for followers. You're most useful back there," Barron ordered. Brashong nodded happily.

"What about us?" Ga asked from beside Sorin, who was perched in a tree.

"Hmmmm, on either side of Ebeny and Camilla," Barron replied. Once everyone was where they were supposed to be, Barron announced, "Let's go."

Sorin flapped to Ebeny's side as Ga zoomed to Camilla. All together they stepped forward and began their journey into the unknown world, certain danger, and even possible death. Camilla had a feeling that they would all get through it together safely if they worked together and if they trusted each other. However, unlike Ebeny, she felt that this would be a *very* long trip.

After trudging along for six hours or so, the tired travelers stopped abruptly. The sight made Ebeny gulp down the urge to yelp. A huge chasm lay in the group's path. The only way across the vast gorge was a bridge that was barely holding together. There were cracked and splintered boards, while some boards were missing altogether. Ebeny shot a fearful glance at Camilla. Camilla, too, was frightened of what lay ahead of them.

«I think it might be a good idea to spread out our weight as much as possible. Too much in one spot may cause those old boards to snap,» Poot suggested.

"Thanks, Poot. That's a good idea. I, personally, would like to stay alive to see the other side of the bridge," Ebeny replied.

"I second that!" Camilla added.

"Redistributing weight is an excellent plan. Let's take some of these packs from Poot and Brashong so we can all share the load across this bridge," Shamoola advised.

Barron and Shamoola went first, then Ga, Brashong, Ebeny, Sorin, Camilla, and lastly Poot. As they walked over the old, rotted, rickety bridge, it swayed back and forth so violently that they were afraid that it would tip and they would fall to their deaths. Slowly, they inched their way across.

The bridge swayed sickeningly, and the queasy feeling in Camilla's stomach increased. Every now and then, a board would creak and everyone would stop. The sound would echo down through the gorge.

Slowly, as members of the group reached the other side, they sighed with relief as both their feet landed on the ground off the bridge. When everyone but Camilla and Poot had made it safely to the other side, they heard a loud *crack*. Camilla let out a high-pitched shriek as the rotted wooden plank she had stepped on gave way under her weight. She felt gravity pull her down, but her hand grabbed onto the bottom rope. Poot looked down at her in shock; her small fingers clung to the bottom rope, horror frozen on her face. Ebeny, Barron, and the rest of the group gasped at the sound of Camilla's frantic scream.

"No, Camilla!" Ebeny tried to race back for her sister, but Barron locked his arms tightly around her stomach. She struggled to get free, but to no avail.

Poot was bending down carefully in order to take hold of Camilla's hand. Suddenly, a board under his foot made a creaking noise. Fear shone in his eyes. He grabbed Camilla's hand and yanked upward. Camilla flew up onto the bridge. Her feet landed safely on the other side of the hole. Poot stepped carefully over the hole and hustled Camilla over the rest of the bridge. They arrived on the other side, both of them out of breath. Everyone sighed with relief. Ebeny ran over and hugged her sister tightly followed by her father and Brashong. "Thanks, Poot. I'd have been dead if it weren't for you," Camilla said. She reached up and hugged him.

«You are quite welcome,» Poot said and wrapped his arms around Camilla to return the hug. The group was silent for a few moments as they reflected on how fortunate they all were to have avoided great tragedy.

Breaking the silence, Camilla quickly pulled her bag off her back and opened it to make sure Squeaker and Sparkle weren't injured. The two were huddled together against the side of the bag, but neither were hurt, just shocked. "It's all right, little guys," Camilla assured them. Then she carefully lifted the two out of the bag and held them close to her. "How would you like to get a little fresh air?" They both nodded.

Ebeny reached out and asked, "How about I carry Sparkle?"

"What do you think, Sparkle?" The little dragon let out a little purr and hopped onto Ebeny's outstretched hand. With a smile, Ebeny gently put the dragon on her shoulder.

The band continued on their journey. The side that they had arrived on looked and sounded as deserted as a desert during midday. Although this forest looked friendly and harmless, Ebeny and Camilla knew better than to judge any forest before they had been through it.

Near sunset, Barron said to stop for the night. Their water supply was extremely low. Sorin did a quick aerial search of the area and reported that there was a stream not too far away where they could replenish their water. Ebeny and Camilla, eager to explore, volunteered immediately to fetch the water.

Barron shook his head. "No. I don't want you going out by yourselves. We don't know where Gorgon has sent his creatures. And gallops aren't the only things you need to watch out for."

"Please, Dad," Ebeny begged.

"Yeah. We can take Brashong with us," Camilla suggested. Brashong, happy that the sisters had chosen him, trotted over to stand by their side.

Barron hesitated before answering. "Well, I suppose you can go as long you take Brashong," He relented. The sisters and Brashong took off in the direction Sorin had pointed to. "Just be back before it gets too dark!" Barron called after them.

The gallop and the two elves, with Sorin's directions, easily found the small stream. Camilla filled a bottle to taste it. She gulped some water then turned to Ebeny.

"It tastes really good," Camilla commented. She handed the bottle to Ebeny, and the younger sister swallowed some with a pleased smile.

"Let's fill these up and go before Dad gets too worried," Ebeny suggested. The sisters did so quickly and were about to turn back when Ebeny asked something unexpected.

"Camilla, would you like to learn the spell that I used at that gallop camp?"

Camilla's mouth hung open in awe. She smiled at her and nodded, quite happy that she had such a wonderful sister.

«Wait, Ebeny,» Brashong said. «Barron wanted us back before it got too dark. Will this take long?»

Ebeny glanced at her sister before saying, "Oh, no. This won't take too long. It's really easy actually."

«Oh, all right then. But don't hurt yourselves,» Brashong agreed.

Ebeny nodded her thanks. "All right, Camilla, the spell that I was talking about is called rashu. All you need to do is say the word, really believe that you can do it, and the power will come flowing into you. Just say it with me." Ebeny walked over to stand beside her sister. Then she pointed at a large pine tree and instructed Camilla to focus all her energy on that spot. Camilla nodded and started to speak the ancient language of the elves.

After at least three tries, Camilla shouted rashu with such power and force that a low branch on the pine in front of her ignited into a bright flame. Camilla gasped while Ebeny's face glowed with pride. Then after a few moments staring at the tree, Camilla turned to Ebeny with a strange look on her face.

"Uh, Ebeny?" Camilla asked hesitantly.

"What?" Ebeny said, still staring at the tree branch.

"What's the spell for water?"

Ebeny's smiled faded. "I don't know."

"We had better use our bottles then," Camilla suggested

"Yeah. After all, we wouldn't want to start a forest fire," Ebeny agreed.

"Or attract any unwanted visitors," Brashong added.

They walked over to the pines with a filled water bottle. They dumped the water onto the branch, and the flame sizzled out. They refilled the watter bottle they had just emptied. Quickly collecting the filled bottles, the sisters and Brashong left the clearing.

As they walked slowly back through the forest, Sorin flew out of the trees and landed casually on Camilla's left shoulder. Ebeny and Camilla smiled at him. Suddenly, Ebeny tripped over a small root sticking up out of the ground.

"Ebeny, are you all right?" Camilla asked, bending down to help her sister.

"Yeah, I'm fine," Ebeny said. She got back up without complaining, but she walked with a limp, and Camilla knew that she was hurt.

"Ebeny, Camilla, Brashong. What took you three so long?" Barron asked as the three reentered the camp. Barron and Shamoola were sitting on the ground with Ga in between them. Poot was over on the fringes of camp but looked over when he heard approaching footsteps. Camilla handed out the water bottles to everyone and returned to Ebeny's side. Ebeny stood tall in an attempt to hide her injured ankle from Barron.

«Ebeny was teaching Camilla the spell she used at the gallop camp,» Brashong explained.

"Really," Barron said. "And how did she do?"

"Pretty well actually," Ebeny answered.

"That's good. I hope you weren't careless when you did it," Barron told them sternly.

"No, we weren't. We filled up our water bottles and had them ready just in case," Camilla assured him.

"Let's just hope no one noticed it. You never know who could be watching in these woods," Barron remarked. The sisters nodded gravely. Brashong went to stand by his brother.

Barron rose from the ground. He announced, "Okay, I think we should get some sleep now."

The tiny group got as comfortable as they could before drifting off to sleep one by one.

Chapter 19

The Dream

The next morning, the group awoke as the first rays of sun began chasing the night away.

"Since we're all awake, we might as well get going," Barron suggested. The rest of the group didn't protest as they gathered their things. They all stood up except Ebeny. Whenever she tried to stand up, she collapsed, saying that her ankle hurt badly.

"You should've told me after you fell, Ebeny. I could have helped you," Camilla told Ebeny, who shook her head.

"I didn't want to be a bother."

Barron walked over and examined Ebeny's ankle. "It looks like it's just a sprain. A little rest and you should be fine, but we can't afford to stay in one place for long."

Brashong trotted over. «Can I help?» he asked.

"Actually, yes. Can you carry Ebeny until we stop again?" Barron asked. Brashong nodded, so Barron carefully helped Ebeny onto the blue gallop's back. Ebeny smiled and held tightly to his waist.

The band continued on its way.

They didn't stop again until sunset.

Just as Barron had predicted, Ebeny's ankle was indeed better. It wasn't fully healed, but she could walk on it without as much pain.

They were all extremely tired from the long day's march, so they turned in early. Everyone fell asleep within minutes of laying down their heads. All of them were sleeping peacefully except for Camilla.

Camilla was twitching and turning on her bed of moss. The moss was all through her mangled hair, and her forehead was drenched with sweat. Underneath her twitching eyelids, a horrid scene was playing before her.

A girl was racing through a dark forest of trees with what felt like never-ending strength and energy. The point that she was focused on ahead of her had a sound coming from it. A blood-chilling, painful moan was coming from before her that gave her strength to keep on running. Camilla knew it was from a friend whom she dearly cared about. This made her to want to know what was causing the deep pain.

All of the trees around her were withering, cracking, and trying to slide away from whatever was making that noise. She was running and running but never seemed to get there. Then, when all hope seemed lost, she burst out of the gloomy forest. In front of her lay nothing, and as she looked down, she saw no earth beneath her feet. It was as if she was floating on air. Camilla was about to turn back when a deep, raspy voice started to speak, *"A friend shall go who is dear to you, but one who is not expected."* The strange voice ended slowly, its last word ringing in Camilla's ears. The voice was like a dreadful thought that only she could hear.

When the echo finally disappeared, Camilla started falling. Down, down, down in a never-ending decent.

Camilla's eyes flew open. She was breathing heavily and, sweat covered her shaking body. Looking around wildly, Camilla was relieved that it was only a bad dream. She thought back to what had happened in the dream. What the voice had said in the dream did frighten her, but it also made her curious. She wondered if there was any truth in the words. She hoped not; she couldn't bear to have any of her friends leave her.

When she turned her head, she saw the sun starting to come up. Despair crept into Camilla. Okay, Camilla, who could it have been talking about? Well, the voice said, "A friend shall go who is dear to you," so it probably doesn't refer to Ebeny or

Barron because it didn't say sister or father. So who among my friends could it have been? Sorin? Maybe. I really do like that runkey. But it also said, "one who is not expected;" what does that mean? She didn't know, but it pained her to even think that Sorin would die.

"Well, would you look at that?" Sorin had emerged out of his nest high in the trees overhead.

Camilla looked where he was pointing and saw Sparkle, the four-winged tiny dragon, flying overhead.

"Wow! Look at you, Sparkle. I guess we don't have to carry you around anymore." The little dragon did a clumsy spiral. Camilla giggled.

CHAPTER 20

A Father's Lesson

"Are we there yet?" Ebeny asked. She was walking between Barron and Camilla, and both of them looked at her and rolled their eyes. "Sorry. I couldn't resist. But really, when are we going to get to the Secret Valley of the Elves?"

"Right now, we're traveling northwest. By the end of the day tomorrow, we should meet up with the Kakeet River. Then all we have to do is follow the river as it bends to the west, and it will lead us to the Saya Mountains, within which lies the Secret Valley of the Elves," Barron explained.

"Well, that doesn't seem too hard to find. What makes it so secret?" Camilla asked.

"Only those who have the elfin touch can enter the valley. Without the touch, a person can wander the Saya Mountains for years and never find the Valley," Barron said.

"The elfin touch? Do we have that?" Ebeny asked.

"Of course you do. You're half elf. I have it, too, because Ariona gave it to me. Good friends of the elves sometimes had the privilege of receiving this gift. King Shamoola has it as well."

"Awesome. But how do we use this elfin touch?" Camilla inquired.

"All you have to do is touch a special spot on the side of the mountain, and the entrance will unlock and magically appear."

"How do we know where this special spot is?"

Barron just smiled and replied, "You'll see when we get there."

The sisters exchanged confused looks. Ebeny reached up and touched her butterfly necklace as they continued to trudge through the woods.

Father and daughters continued to walk side by side in silence for a while.

Around mid-morning, Barron broke the silence. "Ebeny, Camilla, I would like to teach you a spell that might come in handy. I know you already know rashu. This new spell is called disle. It's a shield spell. It protects you from many dangers, but you have to learn how to control it first."

"Great," Camilla said, "I was getting pretty tired of just walking. Can I try it first?"

Barron nodded. "First, you must picture in your mind what you'd like to shield. Start off small—like your hand. Picture an invisible shield wrapping itself around your hand and say the word *disle*."

Camilla took a deep breath and closed her eyes. She imagined her hand being surrounded by a thin bubble. She opened her eyes and said, "Disle." Her right hand shimmered, but otherwise looked completely normal.

Barron nodded happily, but Ebeny didn't seem convinced that the shield spell had worked. She bent down and picked up a stick. She grabbed Camilla's arm and held it out in front of her. She began to hesitantly poke Camilla's hand with the jagged end of the stick.

Camilla looked at her in confusion and asked, "What are you doing?"

Ebeny simply replied, "I wanted to see if the spell worked or not. Did you feel that?"

"No," Camilla said.

"How about this?" Ebeny began to whack Camilla's hand harder and harder with the stick.

Camilla ripped her hand out of Ebeny's grip and hollered, "Stop that!"

Ebeny looked surprised. "Did you feel anything?" She asked again.

Camilla, who was still appalled at what her sister had done, screeched at her, "No! Of *course* I didn't feel anything!"

This surprised Ebeny. She took a step away from Camilla in shock. "Sorry. I just wanted to see if it worked."

"That's okay," Camilla took the stick from Ebeny and held it up menacingly, "Your turn!"

Barron took the stick from Camilla and threw it in the woods. "That's enough, girls."

They heard laughter behind them where the rest of the group was following. "Ah, the love between two sisters is such a beautiful thing. It brings a tear to my eye," Sorin said. Everyone laughed at this, including Barron, Ebeny, and Camilla.

"That was fun. Like you said, Camilla, now it's my turn," Ebeny said.

"Wait a minute. How do I get this shield off?" Camilla asked.

"It's off already. The shield only stays up when you're concentrating on it. When you lose your concentration, the shield disappears," Barron explained.

The girls both nodded in understanding. Then Ebeny took a deep breath and said, "Disle." Her entire left side shimmered.

Suddenly, a nut whizzed through the air and bounced off Ebeny's left shoulder. All three of them turned and looked behind them. Sorin smiled innocently. "What?" Sorin asked, "I just wanted to see if it worked." They all laughed at Sorin while he just bowed his head and looked as bashful as a tiny kitten.

Chapter 21

A Tail as Tall as the Moon

«We are all ready to leave now, sir. All of our belongings have been put away.»

"Wonderful'Poot, thank you for reporting our status." Poot bowed his head and his eyes smiled at Camilla before he turned and left.

Barron, Ebeny, and Camilla rose from their seats at the fringes of camp. Barron strode over to the front of the group while Ebeny walked slowly to Brashong with Camilla close behind.

«Ebeny, would you like a ride again?» Brashong asked.

Ebeny shook her head, "No, thank you, Brashong. My ankle's feeling much better now."

Ga interjected, "Your ankle may be feeling better, Ebeny, but that doesn't mean that it's completely healed."

«Ga is right. You should rest your ankle again today. It's really no trouble for me to carry you again, Ebeny.» Brashong said.

"Well, okay. It couldn't hurt. Thanks, Brashong," Ebeny said with a smile.

Camilla then made a cup with her hands that Ebeny easily put her foot in. She pushed up with her foot and swung her other leg over Brashong's back. Camilla dropped her hands and walked back to Poot.

«Would you like a ride, too?» Poot asked kindly.

"No, thanks. I'm not the one who sprained my ankle. I can walk," Camilla answered.

«It's no trouble—really. Just get on.»

"Well, if you insist, I guess I will. Thanks," Camilla said. Poot kneeled, and Camilla effortlessly got on his back.

Barron pointed forward to tell the group to move on, and Camilla sighed deeply.

«What's wrong?» Poot's right tentacle eye was looking at her with concern.

"Oh, nothing Poot," Camilla replied plainly. "I'm just tired of moving around so much and not having enough time to eat a proper meal. I haven't even had a bath in ages, so I probably smell like a big fat skunk." His eye looked happier and turned back around. Poot's next step was larger than Camilla had expected. It jerked her forward. Two olive hands reached back to steady her. Camilla, with no other way in her head to thank him, quickly patted him on the head. His tentacle eyes turned around and gave her a quizzical look. She shrugged and the tentacles turned back to their normal position.

"Ga," Camilla called softly to the becon floating not too far in front of them. He slowed for them to get close enough for speech.

"What is it Camilla, my dear?" He came closer.

"I have a question. Did you know my mother, Ariona?"

"Yes."

"Will you tell me about her?"

A white light glowed for a second before he spoke. "That's not a question that I should answer. Wouldn't you like Barron to answer that instead?"

Camilla shook her head. "No. I want to hear it from you, Ga. Please."

Ga sighed. "All right, I'll tell you. She loved to laugh. She was also unconditionally kind.

"She was beautiful and incredibly smart, but she was never conceited. She helped out where she was needed without a complaint. Her heart was big enough to hold all of the people in the worlds.

"I first met your mother when I was still teaching. She was my best and brightest student," Ga said.

"What do you mean student?" Camilla asked, absorbed in Ga's story.

"I used to train elves. I taught your mother, but she honestly didn't need me. She was very talented in spells and handling a weapon. I suppose she enjoyed my teachings because I was invited to her and Barron's wedding. I doubt Barron remembers me from that day. He was wrapped up in the festivities. Afterword, Ariona requested that I come for a visit. I did so and was astounded when I saw you in Ariona's arms and wrapped tightly in a blanket. You had such a tiny, sweet face.

"I never knew you well as a baby, but I saw you a few times after that day. All of my friends told me how lucky I was to know Ariona. I couldn't make it to see Ebeny when she was born for I was busy avoiding Gorgon's troops. However, I was eventually forced to join them. I never saw what happened to Ariona in that final battle, but I know she went bravely. The name of your mother will be honored for generations to come."

Camilla had tears in her eyes that she hurriedly wiped away. Trying not to let anyone see, Poot had misty eyes as well. Two mechanical arms shot out from Ga that gave Camilla a comforting hug before he whizzed back off to his regular position, leaving Camilla with Poot at the back of the line.

«That was really nice of Ga to tell you all those things,» Poot said quietly.

"Yeah," was all Camilla could say.

«I wish I had known her. She seems wonderful. You and Ebeny were lucky to have had had such a great mother. And I think she is still here.»

Camilla looked puzzled. "Why?"

Poot's tentacle eyes turned and and looked at her. «From what Ga said, I can see her in you.»

Camilla smiled and leaned forward to give him a hug. His eye stalks straightened happily.

They traveled all day with few breaks. They were trying to reach the Kakeet River by sunset, but as the sun swiftly sank toward the northern horizon, they still had not seen any sign of the river.

Camilla gazed up at the darkening sky. She still wasn't used to the sun setting in the north and not the west. All around her, animals nestled into their nests and burrows, dens and caves. Something chirped lowly in the shadows of big trees, unseen. It would have all been normal for Camilla except for the rustling of eight-footed beings and glimpses of two heads on one neck.

Suddenly, large thumping noises could be heard ahead of them. Something immense, scaly, and frightening stepped out onto the road in front of Barron's path.

Barron scowled and stopped walking. The rest of the group halted. Ebeny and Camilla looked over at each other as fear overtook them. Camilla felt Poot tense beneath her and saw his fists clench. Ahead of her, Barron took a step forward and brought up his hands as sparks began to fly from the tips of his fingers. "Step out of my way or pay the price, danglow," Barron ordered. The creature had massively bulky arms and legs. It was bright yellow with dark black spikes running down its back. Its eyes were dark red with milky white slits in the middle. For a mouth, it had only a circle with two rows of deadly sharp, rotating, yellow teeth. A rather large spike ended a tail that looked tall enough to touch the moon. All along the tail were little nicks as if it had been in many battles and won them with a souvenir. *It has to be a dinosaur,* Camilla thought gravely to herself. Aloud, she called, "Sparkle, come down here!" The little dragon had been flying above her head, but upon hearing Camilla's words, she quickly swooped down and joined Squeaker in the bag on Camilla's shoulder.

As Camilla fastened the flap on her bag, she noticed that Poot was slowly working his way over to his brother. Ga, Sorin, and Shamoola were also edging their way to Ebeny and

Camilla without being detected by the evil danglow's watching eyes. Then the danglow spoke.

"My master, wishes to see you. I will please him." His voice rumbled like thunder and his forked tongue flicked out of his mouth. He crouched low as the beginning of a howl escaped his throat. As he straightened, the howl grew louder and louder. Suddenly, more of the hideous danglows melted out of the woods and joined the howl. Some of them were orange and black, but most were yellow and black like their leader. There were too many for Barron's fire alone. Ebeny met Camilla's eyes. They knew what to do. Camilla bent down and whispered into Poot's ear. He nodded and shared it with everyone else using his mynapathy. They all nodded and circled up. Camilla dismounted and walked nervously to the center of the circle with Ebeny. Then the plan went to work.

Barron thrust his hands out at the gigantic leader of the danglows with red fire shooting out of them crazily. The fire hit the danglow on the shoulder, and it roared in pain. Shamoola drew his sword and slashed madly at two others. Sorin threw rocks that he had picked up from the ground. Poot, Brashong, and Ga shot laser after laser at the remaining three. All of it hardly seemed to affect the hoard of danglows. There was a rustle, and two more came out of the woods.

Camilla shouted over the shooting and howling, "Are you sure we can do this—the shield spell for all of us?"

"It's okay! If we hold hands, I think we can combine our power to create it!" Ebeny held out her hand. Camilla took it and smiled mischievously at her sister. "Ready, on my count!" Camilla said and took a deep breath, "One, two, THREE!" Camilla and Ebeny looked deep within themselves for the power of the ancient elves.

"DISLE!!!" The ground shook, and an enormous blue light erupted from under the girls' feet that covered everyone except the danglows. Everyone inside the blue shield smiled from ear to ear.

The injured leader thrust its spiked tail over its head directly at the shield wall. It rocketed off in another direction and slammed into a tree. At the same time, Poot, Barron, Brashong, and Ga focused their lasers and fired at the hulking creature. Its tail went rigid, and the yellow and black beast collapsed in a senseless heap. Upon seeing their leader defeated, the danglows' faces turned to fear, and melted back into the shadows .

Camilla and Ebeny laughed inwardly, then so loudly it echoed inside the shield. When the girls were sure the creatures had gone, they let the shield drop. Suddenly, they felt exhausted and would have fallen to the ground if not for Barron and Poot coming over to steady them.

"Well, that was fun. Let's do it again," Sorin said optimistically. They all looked at him and laughed. Even Camilla and Ebeny managed a little bit of a giggle.

Shamoola advised. "I don't think that thing is dead. It's just knocked out. We should move on before it regains consciousness. I know the river is close, and we should get to the other side as soon as possible." No one argued with that.

Barron gently lifted Ebeny onto Brashong's back. Camilla was gingerly placed on Poot's back. Barron then whispered quietly into their ears, "You may rest; there are good friends here to protect you." With those comforting words entering their heads, they drifted off into a dreamless sleep while their wonderful protectors watched over them.

Barron took the lead again with Shamoola and Sorin at his sides. Ga was positioned at the back. It was the best circle they could muster around Poot, Camilla, Brashong, and Ebeny. They walked close to each other down Barron's path. The moon was full and lit the way just well enough for him to navigate the trees. No one spoke during their fast-paced walk.

About an hour after the danglow encounter, they finally reached the Kakeet River. It took them a few minutes to find a bridge. The water was high, and the bridge was wet and slightly slippery. Barron didn't hesitate and walked straight onto the bridge. He was closely followed by Shamoola with Sorin on his shoulder. Ga zoomed after them. The sound of the rushing water caused Ebeny to stir and open her eyes. She pushed herself slowly off Brashong's shoulders and stretched leisurely. Once she was done stretching, she stared at the bridge. Brashong moved to stand beside Poot at the water's edge. On Poot's back, Camilla was sitting up and yawning. She looked around, confused at first, but then remembered what had happened.

"Well," Ebeny said sleepily, looking at Poot, "what did we miss?"

«We're getting ready to cross to the other side of the river. Hold on tight.» Poot said to Ebeny and Camilla as his hooves clopped on the wooden bridge. «Thanks a lot, you two. Without you and your shield spell, we probably would've been dead back there,» he added.

Hearing this made Camilla proud that she had saved her friends, but her pride was soon overshadowed by dread. She realized that if she and Ebeny had not acted and created the shield, the prophecy from her dream may have happened that very night. Her mind was filled with dark thoughts of the future as the group moved forward, closer to their destiny.

CHAPTER 22

The Valley

A storm was here. The thunder shook the ground, and lightning lit up the entire sky. The screaming, wild wind whipped the trees around like toys in the mouth of a dog. The sisters knew it was morning due to the dull light lingering in the forest, but the dark clouds prevented any more of the sun to be seen. Rain poured down in sheets on the group of travelers seeking a secret valley.

Barron called orders out blindly behind him. He tugged on a rope. Six pulls answered him back. Barron trudged on through the harsh weather, fighting for every step. He had hoped that such a storm would never cross their path. They trudged on and on until, after what felt like days to Ebeny and Camilla, they stood at the eastern base of the Saya Mountains.

Barron uncertainly walked over to the mountain. He looked for a certain spot, but couldn't find it.

"Can you find it, Barron?" Shamoola yelled through the wind. Barron shook his head. Shamoola nodded and moved up beside him and began to look.

Finally, Shamoola pointed under a large ivy leaf to a discolored circle of rock.

"Thank you," Barron called to Shamoola as he laid his hand gently on the spot of stone. Suddenly, a door began sliding magically open. Everyone gathered closer to see what was happening. Once it was open and had finished moving, they went quickly inside. None of them noticed that the door had swung shut behind them; all of their eyes were gazing forward, amazed at the most beautiful place they had ever set eyes on.

Three enormous mountains stood high surrounding the valley. In the valley, it was dry. It was as if there was a magic shield protecting them from any bad weather. Tall trees stretched up to the bright morning sky. Some of those trees had growing fruit, but some did not. Bushes and shrubs littered the ground. Flowers of all colors surrounded the fringes of the amazing place. Many different winged creatures sat and sang in the tall trees. The clear yellow sun shone down upon a glittering lake.

Barron went around and untied the rope that held the group together. As soon as the rope fell to the ground, Ebeny and Camilla rushed up to the lake. It was magnificently clear and still; they could see their own reflections. A tiny river flowed out of one side. The sisters looked calmly around them. Deep in their hearts, they knew that this was a safe place. It had to be.

Then Camilla spied a line of caves. Most of those caves sat high over the ground. Others sat lower and on the ground. At this distance, Camilla could not see the details, but longed to.

"Ebeny, let's explore those caves," Camilla suggested eagerly.

"All right!" Ebeny agreed happily. Just as the sisters were about to take off, Barron stopped them.

"You may by all means explore the caves, but we need to do it together. We will patrol the area to make sure no one else is here. We'll go in two groups," he ordered. Ebeny and Camilla nodded as they joined Brashong, Ga, and Sorin and began walking toward the other end of the valley. Barron, Shamoola, and Poot went in the other direction.

As they walked, the sisters were astounded at the beauty of the valley. Berry bushes and fruit trees were growing everywhere. They walked to the side of the mountain and followed it around. They passed many caves and checked them to make sure they were empty. The sun rose high in the sky as the groups met up by the lake.

Barron stated, "We are the only ones on the ground. After we eat a quick lunch, we will check the rest of the caves from the ground up." Ebeny and Camilla were ecstatic to be able to see more of the valley but were influenced by the urge to eat.

Poot, Brashong, and Sorin gathered some berries and fruit while Ga and Barron went to check the lake for fish. As they waited, Camilla and Ebeny brought Sparkle and Squeaker out of the bag to play with. When Poot, Brashong, and Sorin brought back the berries and fruit, the girls fed a few berries to Squeaker and Sparkle. Amazingly, when Barron and Ga came back, everyone had a cooked fish to eat. Ebeny wasn't sure about the fish. It had long spikes and small fins that were the color of a bruise. She tried it, discovered it wasn't too bad, and quickly finished the strange fish.

"Are we going to finish checking the caves, Dad?" Ebeny asked, jumping off the ground.

Barron laughed at his daughter's eagerness. "Of course, but you have to wait for the rest of us. And make sure you can still see before coming back down the mountain. I don't want you falling."

"Yes! We will." the sisters shouted together. The two of them along with the rest of the group slowly made their way up a sloping path carved into the face of the mountain. When the path leveled out, they began to check the caves. All were empty. They made their way higher and higher up the mountain. Ebeny and Camilla, even though they were once excited to explore the caves, were now exhausted and relieved when the sun finally set and brought their exploration to a close.

"I see you're tired," Barron remarked as the sisters yawned. They smiled and nodded. "Are the rest of you tired as well?"

Poot and Brashong blinked sleepily and said, "Yes." Sorin nodded as did Shamoola.

"So am I. Let's find a cave big enough for all of us and get some sleep." Barron led the group to one of the larger caves. They fanned out and hunkered down to sleep. Camilla tucked the pets against her side and closed her eyes.

Once they were all situated in the cave, a round of goodnights echoed in the dark. Ebeny moved closer to Camilla and fell into a deep sleep, anxious for morning to come.

As soon as Ebeny and Camilla woke, they decided to explore the caves to a further extent. After checking with their father, the sisters set off for the closest cave and worked their way up the mountain. All of the caves that they revisited had strange writing on the walls. The writing seemed familiar, but they couldn't quite figure out where they had seen it before. Other caves had shelves carved out of the rock face that held ancient jars and boxes full of mysterious items. Some of the caves even had a piece of dusty furniture or two, like a bed or a chair made of wood or carved into the rock.

But one of the caves was very special. Unlike all the other caves, this one had a smaller cave in the back. Around the outside were marks like a beak had been pecking there for a long time. The two girls knelt down in front of the opening. Camilla noticed a word carved above the hole and pointed it out to Ebeny.

"Ingline. I wonder what that is," Camilla said to Ebeny who merely shrugged. Ebeny stood up and was about to suggest leaving the cave when a thought crossed her mind. Her hand reached into her pocket and brought out a folded piece of paper. She unfolded it and scanned it until she finally found what she was searching for.

Kneeling back down by Camilla she said, "No Camilla, not a what, a who." Camilla looked at her questioningly as her sister called into the hole.

"Ingline. Ingline!" There was a shuffling of feet as a small creature appeared out of the darkness. It had slimy skin and feathers all over its small, deformed body. The feathers were nicely preened and white, while the slimy skin was bright green and a bit muddy. Its body was shaped like a frog, but the creature's feet were like chicken feet. Its mouth was a beak that stretched across its face. The eyes were dark brown around a coal black pupil. On top of its head was a beet-red comb, like on any other chicken.

"Wh-who is that?" Camilla asked Ebeny tentatively. Ebeny smiled, and her hand reached out to touch the small creature. When Ebeny came within a foot of its face, the creature cringed away and hopped over to Camilla. Camilla looked surprised but soon warmed up to the small creature.

"This is your pet, Camilla. Her name is Ingline, and mom gave her to you. See, it says so in this letter from her. It was in that box, you know, the one with the freaky writing on it. I can't *believe* I forgot to show it to you. Here." Ebeny handed her sister the letter that she had had with her the entire journey. Camilla took it and slowly read through it. Her eyes widened at the part about the chog.

"I-I can't believe it. This is so cool! She must have known about my loving animals," Camilla said.

"Of course she knew about that. You're her daughter!" Ebeny reasoned.

"Well, yeah, but we didn't stay with her very long, so I didn't know how much she would've known about us."

Ebeny shrugged. "I guess you have a good point there." She paused and smiled. "Let's take Ingline and show her to Barron. I bet he'd really like to see your new pet," Ebeny suggested to her sister.

As they walked down the mountain, Camilla whistled. A purple blur shot down from the sky and landed clumsily beside Camilla's foot. The girls giggled a little at how funny the four-winged dragon looked, her legs sprawled across the ground. Camilla bent down to pick her up and introduce her to Ingline.

"Sparkle, this is Ingline. She's my new pet," Camilla told Sparkle. The dragon nodded and made a purring noise. Camilla set the dragon on her shoulder and continued walking.

"Hey, Camilla. Where's Squeaker?" Ebeny asked.

Camilla shrugged. "I'm not sure. He might be back by the cave entrance eating those berries. By the time we get back, he'll probably have exploded." The sisters smiled. "We should go back for him, though. I don't want him getting hurt or lost," Camilla added and turned to go back up the mountain. Ebeny turned back too, but stopped.

"I guess he beat you to it," Ebeny noted. The chipmunk was sitting in the middle of the path and looking up at Camilla expectantly.

"Good. I was afraid we might not be able to find you. Come on, Squeaker," Camilla said and walked with her sister to the cave where they had slept the night before with Squeaker on her heals. Barron had said to come straight back to that cave when they were done exploring. When they got closer, they heard voices. Camilla guessed that there was a meeting going on. Camilla was just about to tell Ebeny not to go in until they were finished, but Ebeny was already heading into the cave.

"Ah, Ebeny," Barron said from somewhere inside. "Please come in, and bring your sister in as well. I have something to tell you." Ebeny's head popped out of the cave entrance. She motioned for Camilla to come in. She did.

"What is it? Is something wrong?" Camilla tentatively asked when her whole body was standing in front of everyone.

Barron laughed. His laugh was deep. "Why does something need to be wrong for me to want to talk to my beautiful daughters?" Camilla smiled, along with Ebeny. "I just wanted to tell you that Ga and Sorin are going to teach you a bit more magic. There is a cave labeled Training Grotto, and they will set up an area for you to work in." Ga and Sorin flew over to Ebeny and Camilla.

"We'll have some stuff ready for you by tomorrow, so get some sleep. You've been out exploring for a while. Oh and— what is that?" Sorin said, pointing at Ingline.

Camilla looked proud to introduce her new pet. "This," she said slowly after an intake of breath, "is my pet chog, Ingline. She was once my mother's, but now she's mine. Isn't Ingline amazing?" Camilla asked with a smile.

Sorin nodded and said, "She looks loyal, and if this chog was once Ariona's, then I'm sure she'll be a great pet."

"I bet she will be," Camilla agreed.

"Dad, when we were exploring today, we found a cozy little cave not too far from here. Do you mind if we sleep there tonight?" Ebeny asked.

"Sure. I think that will be fine as long as someone else is with you. I'm certain we're quite safe here, but it couldn't hurt to be cautious," Barron said.

"Sorin and I would be happy to stay with Camilla and Ebeny, if they'll have us. We're the ones who are going to wake them bright and early tomorrow morning anyway," Ga suggested.

"That's fine, Ga. Just make sure you don't wake us before the sun comes up," Camilla stated.

"We'll see," Sorin joked.

The sisters smiled, looking forward to tomorrow.

CHAPTER 23

A Memory

Crash! Boom! Clang! Gorgon used his magic to throw yet another piece of furniture against a wall in the main room, expressing his anger. All of Gorgon's servants had left the room in order to avoid Gorgon's temper and all of the flying objects. *Crack!* A wooden table shattered upon impact with the wall. He began to pace once more in front of the cowering Blackess.

"I should've known!" The enraged sorcerer howled. "She escaped. They both did! Argh! How could this happen?"

Gorgon picked up a wooden stand and hurled it at the stone wall. It cracked in two and landed in the growing pile of other broken things.

"It's fine, Master. You couldn't-" Blackess began, his head bowed low and his voice trembling with fear.

"I don't want to hear it!" Gorgon growled. He whipped around to glare at Blackess then went back to his pacing just as quickly.

"Why? Why does it always happen to me? I was so close to having them, so close!" Gorgon complained. He stopped pacing, sighed, and buried his face in his hands.

"Come on, Gorgon, enough screaming. Where would they be headed now? Where?" Gorgon asked himself out loud. He began pacing again, but this time he stopped by the window.

"Barron would lead them somewhere he felt safe. Where would that be?" Gorgon asked himself quietly. He ran his hands through his light brown hair and dropped his arms limply by his sides.

Think. Remember, she told you something one day. Remember ...

Suddenly, Gorgon did remember. He remembered the exact day she told him and where they sat. He remembered what time of day it was and how the sun made her hair look like fire. He remembered the pale, pained look she had on her face as the poison spread through her body...

He dabbed her forehead with a damp cloth. He tried to ignore the pounding of his heart and focus more on the work at hand. She squeezed his other hand as another spasm rocked her frail body. Her strawberry blonde hair was damp from sweat, and he pushed it back from her pale face with the cloth. Her blue eyes were wild from fever. She stared up at him and tried to sit up. Seeing her struggles, Gorgon gently set her upright against the tree behind her.

"Gorgon," she rasped. "You must go to the valley. There is an elf there, a healer named Quant. Tell him what happened. He will give you a powder that will help me." Gorgon shook his head fiercely. "I can't go," Ariona added.

"But I can't either. I'm not an elf. I won't be able to get in. I won't leave you either," Gorgon told her quickly.

"You must, or I will die," she said with a hard stare. "Give me your hand."

"Why?" Gorgon asked.

"I'm going to give you the elfin touch. That's how you can get in."

As Gorgon laid his hand cautiously in hers, he said, "Are you sure?"

Ariona gazed at him and smiled weakly. "Yes, I trust you." Gorgon smiled back at her. She closed her eyes and held his hand tighter. Suddenly, a blue light began to glow around their clasped hands. Along with it, Gorgon felt a tingling sensation and sharp pain, like a shock. As soon as it had started, the blue light was gone, as well as the tingling and the pain.

Ariona opened her eyes. "There," she breathed. "Now you have it."

"Thank you," Gorgon whispered. He looked at his hand, but saw nothing different.

"Now go." She ordered him sharply. "Hurry, before it's too late."

Gorgon nodded nervously and stood. "I'll be back as quickly as possible," he promised.

"I know," Ariona said, as she went through another spasm. She gazed into Gorgon's worried eyes with her feverish ones...

Gorgon gazed out the window. He stared at the tall mountains that surrounded his castle. Their jagged peaks reminded him of three, vine covered mountains far to the north and the valley nestled in the midst of them.

"The Secret Valley of the Elves," Gorgon whispered.

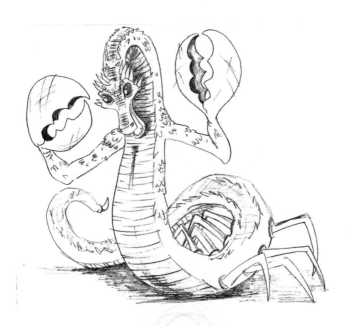

CHAPTER 24

The Training Grotto

"Oh my gosh. This is so cool," Ebeny announced when she and Camilla arrived at the cave marked Training Grotto. Sorin had led them there.

Their eyes slowly scanned the cave, getting used to the lighting. Scattered on the floor were swords and arrows. They saw a small table with two simple swords on it . On the metal part of the swords were engraved in big loopy letters, *Camilla* and *Ebeny.* On the hilt of the swords were many small butterflies. Their wings were in perfect proportion. The pale colors of blue, green, and silver decorated the curving, detailed wings. There were also two bows that had ivy engraved all over the upper and lower limb. The arrows had silver heads that looked like ivy leaves and bright orange feather fletching. Beside the table, three cloth dummies sat against the side wall and against the back wall was a wooden bull's-eye.

"I thought that while we practiced your magic skills, we could also do a few other things in between. As you can see over here we have your ash bows, and over here we have your steel swords. I collected some sturdy sticks too, until you can handle a sword with ease."

"When did you do all this, Ga? After all, we only found out about this yesterday," Camilla asked him. She looked away from the enchanting bows to gaze at her friend.

"It actually didn't take very long to create your bows. It didn't even take that long to etch the ivy leaves on your bows. My lasers come in handy sometimes."

"What about the swords?" Ebeny asked.

"I did not make those. I couldn't have made the engravings in color. Shamoola brought them along. They were made especially for you by the blacksmith Froghorn, who presented them to each of you on your first birthday. He told me that I was to give them to you when we first started training."

Ebeny walked over and carefully touched the hilt of the sword. "Go ahead and pick it up," urged Ga, "After all, it's yours."

Ebeny tentatively wrapped her fingers around the hilt and lifted the sword. "Wow. I thought it would be really heavy, but it's not. It's perfect!"

She started to swing the sword in arcs through the air in front of her. Sorin jumped back a few feet and covered his head, "Whoa! Hold on, Ebeny! I would like to keep my head attached to my body, thank you very much!"

"Sorry, Sorin." Ebeny gently laid the sword back on the table where Ga had it.

"May I suggest that you stick to sticks for now until you get a few lessons?" Sorin said.

"Wise words, runkey," Ga said.

"These are beautiful bows, Ga. Thank you so much. How do we know whose is whose?" Camilla asked.

"The one is a bit longer than the other. That longer one is yours, Camilla." Camilla nodded and gently wrapped her hand around the middle of the wooden part of the bow. She ran her fingers delicately down the string and lightly traced some of the ivy leaves etched in the wood.

"It's perfect," she whispered quietly to no one but herself. She placed the bow down cautiously before walking over to Ebeny.

"Thank you, Ga. These are beautiful," Camilla told the becon hovering next to her.

"Yeah, thanks a lot, Ga," Ebeny added thoughtfully.

"You are quite welcome, my dears. You would have needed them sooner or later." He paused before speaking again. "All right, now it is time for me to tell you about my holographic device. It allows me to produce a hologram of whatever I want. My hologram can stand still, or it can move around on its own. For example, attacking bambargle..." Ga's lights shut off and an odd whirring sound came from him.

Suddenly, in front of them sprung a ten-foot-tall hologram of a bambargle. It had the body of an orange snake with eight rather small but strong legs. In the middle section were two huge crab pincers. Each of the pincers was at least three mailboxes long. Its head was a snake's head, but it had spikes sticking out on both sides. The thing's eyes were like dark black beads that had the smallest of small pure white pupils.

"Well, what do they do now, Ga?" Sorin asked, a little shaky. Ga's eyes came back on and into focus.

"I will tell Ebeny or Camilla a spell to use on this hologram. Once the attacking spell, such as rashu, hits the bambargle, the hologram takes control of the energy and uses it to make itself look battered and dead. However, the hologram will only do that if it is the right spell." He finished speaking and gazed around expectantly at them. He sounded very proud of the explanation of his holographic device.

"Well," Ga said, "let's start with what you already learned. It was the rashu spell, wasn't it?" He paused long enough for Ebeny and Camilla to nod their heads. Then he started to speak again.

"Camilla can go first. Then Ebeny, you follow. Back up a little, please. I don't know how powerful you are yet, and I don't want this holographic device to break. It took a long time to track down all of the parts that were necessary." Sorin led them to a small line in the dirt that he had made for them while Ga was speaking. Camilla walked to the front of the line, as Ebeny strode in behind her.

"All right, let's see you work your magic. Camilla, please go first to enlighten us. Ebeny has already done this a few times, but she still needs practice," Ga instructed.

"Okay," she whispered. Ga got into position and mumbled something to himself. A large gallop burst up in front of her. Reacting to this startling sight, Camilla hollered, "Rashu!" Her arms flew forward, and the on-coming gallop fell down in pain from a smoking gash on its side. Camilla's face glowed with delight.

"I'm ready, Ga," Ebeny told the becon. In response, he shut off and out leapt a gigantic bambargle. This one was bigger than the one Ga had shown them earlier. Then something unexpected happened. Instead of acting as if it were attacking, the bambargle disconnected from Ga. The becon's eyes immediately turned on.

"Ebeny, just destroy it! The bambargle got too strong so it got away from me. If you don't stop it, it will go rampaging through this valley and destroy everything in its path." Ebeny was stunned, but she was roused by Ga and Sorin's voices yelling, "Ebeny! Ebeny! Ebeny!" She stared at the monster in front of her. Ebeny got ready to defend herself. She held her hands up in front of her and her palms began to glow red in preparation of the spell rashu. The bambargle's beady black eyes seemed to be drilling holes into her face and extremely unnerved her.

The bambargle looked warily at Ebeny's bright palms. Then, suddenly, the bambargle turned to face Camilla and quickly advanced on her. Camilla was shocked into silence, but only for a few seconds.

Glancing at her sister Camilla yelled, "Ebeny, together?"

Ebeny nodded.

"One, two, three, rashu!" Camilla shouted. Ebeny joined in, and their power together destroyed the bambargle.

Sorin and Ga were stunned but quickly came out of it.

"Girls, that was amazing!" Sorin shouted.

"I agree. You two are quite talented," Ga added.

"Thanks," the sisters said together.

"I am quite sorry about that bambargle. My holographic device must have something wrong with it, but it isn't anything that I can't fix." Ga apologized. "Now on to the other things we need to do. After what we saw with that pack of danglows, I think you can already master disle, which means we don't have to review that. Sorin and I will teach you two new spells. I will take Camilla first, and Sorin will take Ebeny. When both girls have mastered that spell, we will switch, and Ebeny will go with me, while Sorin takes Camilla." They nodded and separated. Sorin took Ebeny toward the entrance as Ga led Camilla toward the back of the cave.

Sorin stopped and nodded to Ebeny when she caught up with him. "Let's get started. I'm going to teach you linka, the light spell. Try it first. Then we'll try and control the light," he said.

Ebeny took that as her cue to begin the light spell. She nodded and said, "Linka." A dull white glow emanated from her hands but blinked out quickly.

"Go ahead and try again," Sorin instructed. "This is a spell that requires a lot of energy, but is simple to perform."

Ebeny took a deep breath before saying in a quiet but powerful voice, "Linka!" This time, a bright white light spread across Ebeny's body, making her almost impossible to see. In the middle of her chest where the butterfly necklace was, a bright blue light shone out. What you could see of Ebeny were her eyes, tightly shut, and her hands that were balled into fists. Suddenly her eyes flew open and out poured a blue light. The source of the light was the exact middle of Ebeny's light blue eyes. At the same time her eyes came open, her hands unclenched as well. From the center of her sweaty palms a pale light shone out onto the rock face. Her eyes and hands shot out beams of light like the beacon in a lighthouse. During this, Sorin was temporarily blinded. Hiding behind his wing was all he could do to stop the glare from getting to his eyes.

This all lasted for about thirty seconds before Ebeny gave out and began to sway. She stuck out her arm to steady herself, forcing herself to breathe evenly. Lowering herself slowly, Ebeny sat down on the cool cave floor. Sorin hopped up onto Ebeny's sagging shoulder.

"Wow, Ebeny. That was the brightest light I've seen anyone do on their first time," Sorin exclaimed. Ebeny nodded. Sorin sighed, realizing how tired Ebeny really was. Her eyes were the only part of Ebeny's body that didn't look as if all the life had seeped out. Her eyes were lively and sparkling with happiness from Sorin's compliment.

Meanwhile, at the back of the cave, Camilla was doing a completely different spell.

"Now, Camilla," Ga began, as he picked up a stick with his mechanical hand, "I am going to teach you mitle, the disarming spell. Be warned; this will probably tire you out very quickly. All spells use up energy, but some spells use more than others. You must learn which spells those are and when to use them."

"Okay. I'll remember that," Camilla said. "Mitle." Camilla was disappointed to see nothing happened.

"It's all right, Camilla. It's difficult to perform a spell perfectly the first time. Try again," Ga advised.

"Mitle," Camilla said it a commanding voice. She was delighted to see the stick try and escape from Ga's grasp.

"Wonderful, Camilla," Ga praised her.

An immense smile crossed her face. "Thanks, Ga! But I know I can do a lot better."

Ga chuckled. "I'm sure you can. Just don't push yourself. It's not good for someone just learning magic. Go ahead and try the spell again."

Camilla nodded and took a deep breath. "Mitle," she said. This time Camilla's voice rang with the same powerful cadence as Ebeny's voice did when she had done linka. Ga heard this difference and tightened his grip on the stick he was holding. It made no difference whatsoever. The stick flew across the room and hit the rock wall with a sharp *crack!* Ga stared at his empty hand and then at Camilla's face. *He looks so proud!* Camilla remarked. *I must've done it right.*

"That was fantastic, Camilla. Try it once more, but this time," Ga added as Camilla took a deep breath again, readying herself, "try to control where the stick goes when it flies out of my hand."

Camilla looked uncertain. "Um, how do I do that exactly?" she asked.

"As you are saying mitle, think left, right, up, or down, whichever way you want it to go. Do you understand?" Ga explained.

"I think so," Camilla assured him. She closed her eyes and thought, *left,* as she said loudly, "Mitle." The stick instantly flew out of Ga's hand to the left and collided with the wall.

Camilla whispered, "Yes!" and wiped a bead of sweat from her forehead.

"Astounding, Camilla. For your first time, this is amazing progress. Do you want to try sending the stick two directions?" Ga inquired.

"If you think I'm ready," Camilla answered, but her face said differently.

"Of course you are. Try thinking the directions right, then up. All right?" Ga reassured her.

Camilla nodded. "All right," *Right, up,* she thought. "Mitle!" Camilla shouted. The enchanted stick obeyed and flew right, then up, hitting the ceiling and breaking in half. Camilla was ecstatic, but very tired. She was breathing hard and understood what Ga had said about spells taking a lot out of you. She leaned against the cold, stone wall.

"Well done, Camilla. I would ask more of you, but I don't want to exhaust your powers. Is that all right with you?" Ga said. Camilla didn't speak; she simply nodded.

"Sorin!" He called across the cave. The runkey turned to look at him. "I think we should take a bit of a break. These girls are tired, and I don't want to push them."

"I agree," Sorin shouted back. "Do you want me to bring Ebeny over?"

Ga looked at Camilla nodding her head. "Yes, that would be nice," he decided.

"Thanks, Ga," Camilla said as she stood up and waited for Ebeny to arrive.

When she did, both girls collapsed onto the ground. They immediately began talking about what they'd been doing and how well they did. Camilla highly congratulated Ebeny on her bright light. Ebeny did the same for Camilla. While they were doing that, Ga and Sorin were explaining their experiences as well.

All too soon for Ebeny and Camilla, Ga ordered, "All right, I think it's time to get back to training." Camilla said nothing and stood up, unlike her sister.

"Aw, come on, Ga. Just five more minutes?" Ebeny pleaded, much to Camilla's amusement.

"Come along, Ebeny. Your sister is eager to learn, and Sorin won't start teaching her until I've started with you. You'll like the spell I'm going to teach you. I promise," Ga coaxed.

Ebeny looked at Camilla's pleading face and relented. "Well, okay. Let's get started." Sorin nodded and led Camilla away.

"Are we just staying here, Ga?" Ebeny asked. Ga nodded his agreement while staring intently at Camilla. Ebeny cleared her throat loudly. Ga shook himself and started to teach.

"Now, I realize that you are quite tired, Ebeny. I won't expect too much from you, all right?" Ga told her. She nodded.

Ebeny paid close attention to everything Ga said or did. Ebeny performed the spell mitle just as well as linka, even though she was extremely tired. All of the sticks that Ga was holding flew out of his steel, mechanical hand. Ga nodded approvingly.

"Ebeny," Ga said. "I want you to try controlling where the stick goes by thinking either right, left, up, or down." Ebeny nodded. She glanced mischievously at Sorin and thought, *Far right, stick.* "Mitle!" She shouted with the magnificent sound that only came when using magic.

The stick flew out of Ga's hand and across the cave where it bounced off Sorin's head. Sorin fell to the ground and then looked over in surprise at Ebeny. "I thought we agreed that you weren't going to hurt me today, Ebeny," Sorin reminded her.

"Oops. I guess I forgot," Ebeny replied with a mischievous smile. Then she began laughing so hard she had to lean against the wall for support. Camilla and Ga started to laugh, too.

"Oh, great. Let's all laugh at the injured runkey. Splendid idea," Sorin commented sarcastically. But then even he couldn't stop the grin that crept over his face.

As soon as Ebeny got her breath back, she apologized to Sorin with a big smile on her face. The runkey accepted and returned to teaching Camilla.

"Now, Ebeny," Ga began. "I can see you can control the stick, but we are still going to practice it a few more times. I would appreciate it if you didn't hit Sorin anymore, no matter how appealing the idea may seem to you." Ebeny nodded and completed her time with Ga.

When both girls were finally done with all their training, darkness was creeping up into the cave and onto the exhausted sisters. Sorin announced the lateness of the hour and suggested that they head back to their cave for the night. The small group turned their heads to look at the magnificent sunset. Orange, yellow, navy blue, purple, and pink filled the eastern horizon, and wisps of white, wandering clouds decorated the now darkening sky. To the exhausted Camilla and Ebeny, it was the best sight they had seen all day. They had enjoyed learning from their two closest friends, but they were terribly tired and wanted to go to sleep.

Ga stuck a hand out and laid it on Camilla's shoulder gently. Camilla turned away from the marvelous sunset before her to look up at Ga and smile. He looked down and smiled back. "Well," Ga said after a few moments of silence, "we had better get some sleep, especially you two," he said, looking playfully at Ebeny and Camilla, whose shoulder his hand still rested lovingly on.

When the little group finally reached the cave, Ebeny and Camilla dropped on the floor. They got themselves comfortable on their separate sides on the cave: Ebeny and Camilla on one side, Sorin and Ga on the other. Ga turned a dull light on underneath him to look for a place to hover that wasn't close to the wall.

Before going to sleep, Camilla and Ebeny talked in quiet voices. Ga had marvelous hearing and caught many words and phrases that the sisters exchanged. The last few sentences Camilla and Ebeny exchanged were the most meaningful. "Tomorrow is my thirteenth birthday. Can you believe I'm going to be a teenager?" Camilla asked.

"No, I can't," Ebeny replied. "You're getting so old. Should I have Ga make you a cane?"

Camilla laughed. "No, I'm good. Good night, Ebeny," Camilla whispered with a smile.

"Night," Ebeny replied.

After that, the sisters curled up with their backs against the wall, and fell asleep.

Although the cave was silent, Ga's head whirled with plans and ideas for the next day as he fell into a deep, dreamless sleep.

Chapter 25

A Birthday

"**W**ake up, sleepy head!" Camilla's eyes flew open; her body was drenched in sweat. As she stared at Ebeny, fear pulsed though her wide green eyes. During the night, she had had the terrible prophecy of death for a close, unexpected friend again. She was too frightened to tell anyone about her dreams. Ebeny's observant eyes caught the lingering fear in her sister's eyes.

"You okay, Camilla?" Ebeny reached out to help her up. Camilla met her sister's worried eyes, and all fear trickled out of them as she took hold of the offered hand.

"Yeah, I'm fine. Just a bad dream," Camilla explained quickly.

She jumped up as Poot suddenly entered the cave, startling Camilla. They walked over to join him at the entrance.

«Good morning, you two. I was wondering if I could borrow Camilla for a while. I wanted to talk with her while seeing the whole area of the Secret Valley of the Elves. Is that all right with you?» Poot asked. Ebeny nodded and pushed Camilla forward, for she knew what was going to happen when her sister was gone.

"Yeah, go on, Camilla. You'll have fun," Ebeny encouraged.

"Well, I guess," Camilla said. Poot knelt down low to make it easier for Camilla to climb onto his back. She did so with the ease of practice. Ebeny waved to Camilla and Poot until they were lost from sight.

Then Ebeny skipped away to join Sorin and Ga. They had wanted to see her early on, but Ebeny wanted to see if Camilla was awake first. She met them where Barron had said the Kakeet River started to flow.

When she arrived at the cluster of trees by the river, she saw Sorin and Ga were just finishing a ragged looking table. Barron, Shamoola, and Brashong were just arriving with vines and flowers.

"Hi, guys. I'm here," Ebeny said.

Without turning around, Ga said, "Hello, Ebeny. Let us just finish this table, and then we can talk." Ebeny nodded and sat down on a moss-covered rock nearby.

Finally, Ga and Sorin were finished. They flew over to her and sat down.

"Well, is she gone?" Ga asked uneasily.

"Yeah. Poot took her just before I got here," Ebeny confirmed.

"That's good. Barron, Shamoola, Poot, and Brashong pitched in and are helping us. Barron and Brashong are collecting flowers and vines to decorate what we can. You and Sorin are going to go and collect some fruit. I saw some paffleberry and jingberry bushes as well as apple trees near where we entered the valley. They will make a lovely assortment for Camilla. Shamoola and I will go try to catch some fish in the lake. Sparkle, Squeaker, and Ingline will help you, Ebeny," Ga informed her.

He nodded to Sorin and Ebeny and zoomed off. Ebeny whistled for the pets. They came quickly from under the table.

"Let's go collect some berries," Sorin said enthusiastically. He handed Ebeny a box. "I found it in a cave and cleaned it out. We'll use it to put the fruit in." He led Ebeny to the berry bushes and fruit trees. They picked nonstop with the pets pushing the box to where Ebeny and Sorin were picking. When the box was full, Sorin and Ebeny carried it back to the cluster of trees.

Ebeny put the box down and gently poured the berries onto table. There was a tub of water already sitting on the table. Ebeny assumed ga had put it there to wash the fruit. Barron and Brashong were trying to hang up the vines and flowers nicely, but the decorations ended up looking odd and out of place. Barron turned and noticed Ebeny and her crew.

"Ah, good. These plants could use a woman's touch," Barron joked. Brashong smiled at her and handed her a pink and blue polka-dotted flower with leaves shaped like five-pointed stars. Barron laid down a long lime-green vine that he had failed to hang right. Ebeny put the flower down and hung up the vine perfectly, putting the men to shame. Brashong went over to the table and began helping Sorin,

Sparkle, Squeaker, and Ingline to clean up the berries and apples. Barron helped Ebeny hang up the vine and flowers. Soon, Ga and Shamoola arrived with a bin of rather large fish and they began cooking the fish. Brashong and Sorin worked on a smiling face made of the apples on the table and Camilla's name made of the berries.

Finally, the decorations and the food were ready. It wasn't fancy, but they were all sure that Camilla would love it. Flowers and vines covered the place beautifully. They finished just in time; Poot was galloping close enough for them to just make out his shape. Ebeny had them stand around the ash table to hide the fruit and smoking hot fish. Poot and Camilla arrived in a few minutes. Poot stopped in front of the anxiously await-ing group and kneeled down for his rider to leap onto the ground. Camilla's smile was replaced by a look of curiosity.

"What are you doing?" Camilla was truly baffled by the scene in front of her eyes. Smiles from ear to ear covered the faces of the party planners., They jumped aside while yelling happily, "Surprise!! Happy birthday!" Camilla took one look at the plain looking food and cried. Not from sadness, but from the great joy that flooded through her. Ingline and Squeaker crowded around Camilla's feet. Sparkle flew over from Ebeny's shoulder to land on Camilla's and nudged Camilla lovingly. Ingline and Squeaker sat happily on Camilla's shoe. Ebeny ran over to Camilla and held her in a hug so tight that it hurt. The younger sister stepped back beside the rest of her friends.

"Wow, how much trouble did you go through to do all of this?" Camilla asked.

Sorin spoke up from Barron shoulder. "Ah, it was a piece of fruit cake!" They all laughed at Sorin's joke.

"It was all Ga and Barron's idea," Ebeny said.

«It was your idea as well, Ebeny,» Brashong added. Ebeny shrugged and blushed a little as she fingered Ariona's butterfly necklace that was warm from sitting on Ebeny's skin.

Barron walked over and laid a hand on Camilla's shoulder. "Those beautiful swords of yours and Ebeny's do need something to hold them in. These were made right after the swords by Froghorn. Shamoola and I have been saving these for you ever since we left the castle." He walked over to a little patch of ferns and pulled out two scabbards. They were both light brown. A shining bronze belt buckle was on one end of each of the scabbards while the other end was curved and had six holes near the end. The sisters thanked Barron and Shamoola many times and stood back to admire the scabbards as everyone sang to Camilla. They then consumed Ga's admirable fish and devoured the fruit and berries. They hung around that spot for a while, talking, laughing, and enjoying each other's company. Camilla and Ebeny sat and giggled along with their best friends, who were all practically family, not having a care in the world.

After they had cleaned up all their leftover trash, they split up. The exhausted sisters led Ga and Sorin back to their cave with Ingline, Sparkle, and Squeaker trailing behind. Barron and Shamoola walked back to their cave, talking the whole way. Brashong and Poot ran around the valley a few times before finally going to rest in their separate cave.

Back in the sisters' cave, Ga and Sorin were comfortable and asleep, but Ebeny and Camilla were lying awake replaying the day's events. Finally, they curled up beside each other and began to drift off into sleep.

"Happy birthday, Camilla," Ebeny said just before she slipped into a deep sleep.

"Yeah," Camilla replied. "It sure was."

CHAPTER 26

hidden Skills

"Yes!" Ebeny shouted when she received the good news. The sisters were sitting on the floor in the Training Grotto when Ga announced their training plan for the day. "Finally, we get to use the swords."

"And bows. You can't forget the bows and arrows," Camilla added.

"Yeah, those too," Ebeny amended.

"But we can't start until Sorin gets here," Ga ordered.

Right on cue, the runkey flew into the cave and landed on the floor. "Sorry I'm late. I was taking a short flight around the valley and I lost track of time," he explained.

"It's okay, Sorin," Ebeny assured him with a smile. "At least you're here now. I can't wait to use the swords today!"

"And bows," Camilla added with as much enthusiasm as her sister.

"Great, just don't chop me up, Ebeny. I'm too beautiful to die," Sorin ordered.

They all laughed.

"Wonderful," Ga announced. "Now we can get started."

The girls picked themselves up off the ground and followed Ga and Sorin over to the table that held the beautiful weapons.

"Now," Ga said once Camilla and Ebeny had picked up their swords and were ready, "These training dummies were here when we arrived. They are made of a special material that allows you to stab it repeatedly without dulling the blade. I want you to attack them." He pointed to three lumpy dummies that looked to be made out of cloth. Their arms and legs were made of the same material but were not stuffed. A red X was where the heart would be.

"And make sure that your hit is accurate. In a real battle, if you only cut an arm or something, whoever it is could still kill you," Sorin added. Ebeny and Camilla held back a grimace and nodded.

Ga then told the sisters, in great detail, how to control their swings, the technique of sword fighting, where the deadly hits were, and what to do when certain things happen. Ebeny and Camilla were listening intently and understood everything. They were anxious to start actually practicing with the swords.

Finally, after lots of explaining and teaching, it was time to practice what they had now learned. Ga picked up a sword from the ground and stood behind the dummy. Using his long, mechanical arm, he was going to try to parry their blows like a real enemy would.

"Ready?" Ga asked Ebeny who nodded with excitement. Ebeny began to attack the dummy, but Ga parried her thrusts.

"Quicker," Ga ordered and Ebeny did just that. She moved her sword quicker and put more power in her thrusts.

"Better," Ga commended.

Ebeny grunted and heaved her sword at the dummy's chest. She knocked Ga's sword out of the way and stabbed the X. Ebeny sighed with relief. "Finally," she murmured.

"Good, Ebeny. Now, let's see what your sister can do," Ga challenged. Ebeny stepped back and Camilla moved in front of the dummy. Camilla nodded to Ga and they began. Camilla took a few more tries than Ebeny to stab the X on the wood, but eventually she hit it.

Each time the sisters fought, they became better and more at ease with the weapon, but Ebeny was exceptional. At one point, when Ebeny went against Ga, both Ga and Sorin looked surprised when Ebeny drove her sword point almost straight through the thick plank of wood right on the X marked for the killing blow. The runkey and becon congratulated Ebeny enthusiastically. Ebeny blushed as Camilla gave her a quick hug.

It went on like this for awhile. Even when the X was almost impossible to get at, Ebeny hit it perfectly, and Camilla wasn't too far off. Ga and Sorin soon started to put things in the way of the swinging blades, but Ebeny's sword still hit her target.

"All right," Ga said after training with swords for a few hours, "it's time to switch weapons. I did promise Camilla that we would practice with the bows today, didn't I?" Camilla's head bobbed up and down excitedly. However, Ebeny didn't look as happy. She had enjoyed using the swords.

"I guess," Ebeny muttered in a sour tone. "They don't look nearly as exciting as the swords were."

"Don't worry, Ebeny," Camilla assured her eagerly. "The bows and arrows are going to be great!" Ga nodded.

Ebeny and Camilla retrieved their bows from the table and followed the becon to a large wooden circle with ten rings, one inside the other, with a bull's-eye in the middle. Ga explained to the sisters how to hold the bow, how to nock the arrow, how to pull the bowstring back, and how to smoothly release the bowstring.

Once she got the feeling of how to handle the bow, Camilla hit the center of the bull's-eye every time. Ebeny did well, too, but she didn't hit the bull's-eye nearly as consistently as her sister.

"Wow!" Camilla exclaimed. "The bow is so easy to use. I love it! What about you, Ebeny?"

Her sister shrugged. "Yeah, I suppose, but the sword was way better."

"No way," Camilla disagreed.

"Yes way," Ebeny argued.

"Don't waste time arguing. You both have a weapon that's best for you. Ebeny excels at the sword, while you, Camilla, are clearly an expert at the bow. Now let's get back to practicing," Sorin interjected before Camilla and Ebeny could say anymore.

"Yes, let's set up a little challenge," Ga suggested. "Sorin and I are going to set up a course outside that only the best archer could complete. Camilla, you and Ebeny wait here until I call."

"Okay," Camilla said.

"Hurry up, you two!" Ebeny urged.

"Gosh, Ebeny. You really like challenges, don't you?" Camilla asked with a smile.

Ebeny laughed. "Is it really that obvious?" The sisters sat and laughed with each other, enjoying the moment.

Finally, Camilla heard Ga say, "We're ready!" She jumped up and ran out of the cave to him with Ebeny on her heels. They skidded to a stop and stared at the long space before them. It was at least half the length of a football field. At the end of the course were ten circles that looked like a bull's-eye drawn on a plank of wood.

"We're supposed to hit that?" Ebeny asked in awe. Camilla was at a loss for words.

"If you are as good as I think you are," Ga began.

"Then of course you can do it," Sorin finished curtly. The sisters smiled at their teachers' positive attitude.

"Yeah we can do this," Camilla said.

"Definitely," Ebeny agreed. "Do we get three tries?"

"Sure, Ebeny," Sorin approved through his laughter.

"Great. Go ahead, Ebeny. You can go first," Ga stated.

Ebeny nodded and picked up her bow. She eased her left hand onto the grip and her right hand on the string with the arrow in between her pointer and middle finger. Ebeny slowly pulled back her string as she inhaled. She closed one of her eyes and fixed her aim so her arrow wouldn't go anywhere but the center of her target. As she exhaled, her hand released her string, and the arrow shot forward. The world around them seemed to stand still as the arrow rocketed through the air. It hit the target's third ring, sunk deep into the wood and stayed there, quivering.

Ebeny sighed, clearly relieved. "That wasn't too bad," she admitted. Camilla's proud smile showed Ebeny that her statement was relatively true. Looking at Sorin and Ga, she saw that they, too, had pleased looks on their faces.

"Wonderful, Ebeny," Ga congratulated her. His lights blinked continuously to show his happiness.

Sorin flew over and landed on Ebeny's shoulder. "That was great, Ebeny!" He exclaimed before flying back over to his perch on the rock face.

The young elf grinned. "Thanks, Sorin."

Ebeny tried to hit the bull's-eye two more times. Each time she was better. On her last try, Ebeny hit in between the middle of the target and the first ring.

"Camilla," Ga called. "It's your turn."

Camilla said nothing, but nodded and stepped forward with her bow in hand. She took up her stance and wrapped her fingers around the grip of the bow. She pulled the bowstring back and prepared to release the arrow. Camilla took a deep breath in, and as she exhaled slowly, she released the bowstring, which sent the arrow flying. It flew much faster than Ebeny's had and stopped with a solid thud on the first ring. A vast smile covered Camilla's face,.

Ga said nothing. He simply stared intently at his student and looked back to the target. Camilla took this as a motion for her to continue. She again set up and pulled the string back to the corner of her mouth. Her hands were completely still and suddenly they let free the speeding arrow, which hit right at the edge of the bull's-eye on the target.

"Geez, Camilla,'" Ebeny shouted. "That was a great shot!"

"Thanks," Camilla muttered, not really hearing the compliment her sister had given, for she was already setting up for her last try. *Come on, Camilla. You can do this. Right to the center of that bull's-eye,* Camilla thought as she tried to relax and focus. She inhaled deeply, then let her breath out slowly as she let go of the bowstring. The arrow shot forward and zipped through the course. Camilla gasped when the arrow hit its designated mark, the center of the bull's-eye.

An awed silence filled the Training Grotto and its inhabitants. Then Ebeny broke the silence.

"Wow. Camilla, that was amazing!" Ebeny highly congratulated her sister. She ran over and hugged the stunned Camilla, who was as still as a statue.

As soon as reality sunk in, Camilla blinked and asked quietly, "Whoa. Is that *my* arrow?"

"That was absolutely astounding, Camilla!" Sorin exclaimed with a smile on his face. He flew round and round Camilla's head laughing quietly to himself in sheer joy.

"Camilla, that was unbelievable. Outstanding shot," Ga added. Camilla could hear the pride in his voice.

Once the excitement died down, Camilla noticed the becon studying her carefully, and then Ebeny. *I wonder what he's thinking,* Camilla thought uneasily. As if he had read her mind, Ga spoke in a concerned tone beside Camilla.

"Camilla, Ebeny, you look tired. Why don't we stop for the day?"

At that point, Camilla realized that her burst of energy had disappeared entirely, leaving an exhausted elf in its place. She wiped the sweat from her forehead with the back of her hand. Camilla looked back at Ebeny and met her sister's eyes.

"You know Ga," Camilla began. "I think you're right. This battle training is way harder than I thought."

"Definitely," Ebeny agreed full-heartedly.

Sorin laughed. "I guess I can second that," he announced cheerfully.

"Great. Let's go over to Barron and report our status. How does that sound?" Ga asked.

"Yeah!" The sisters said together.

Ga laughed in his mechanical voice as he led the way to Barron's cave. Ebeny and Camilla followed him, with Sorin in their wake.

Finally, the weary training group stepped inside Barron's cave. They looked around, but didn't see anyone. Ebeny began to worry if something had happened to her father.

"Now, what do we have here?" A big voice asked from behind them. "Are you looking for me?" Ebeny and Camilla turned around. Barron stood behind them tall and proud.

"Yes," Ga answered. "We just finished for the day, and I thought you'd like to know the sisters' progress. Do you?"

"Of course!" Barron said with enthusiasm. "How well are you doing? You're telling me because they are doing well, right?" he asked, suddenly worried.

Sorin laughed. "They are actually doing extraordinarily well." He winked at Ebeny as Ga blinked at Camilla proudly. Both of the girls blushed deeply.

Barron grinned and asked, "What did you teach them today, Ga?"

"Swords and bows," he answered quickly.

"When did you start?" Barron inquired with a confused look on his face.

"Just after the sun came up."

Barron looked flabbergasted. "What? And you're done so soon?"

Ga nodded. "Yes. They were amazing; they adapted to the different techniques unnaturally quickly. It was astounding."

"Yes," Sorin agreed as he flapped onto Barron's shoulder, "Now they're almost as good as I am!"

Everyone laughed. The joyful sound echoed through the peaceful valley.

As the merry group was laughing, Shamoola walked in behind them.

"What's going on here?" Shamoola asked. "Shouldn't Ebeny and Camilla be training?"

"Shamoola, my friend, that is the very same question I asked myself. There is a good explanation for this, believe me," Barron reasoned.

"Then let me hear it," Shamoola agreed, and he walked further into the cave to stand by his old friend.

Barron and Sorin looked at Ga, and the becon explained what had happened in the day's training session.

Shamoola looked stunned. "Really?" Ga and Sorin both nodded. Shamoola looked at the sisters who were blushing intensely again. Shamoola said, "Wonderful, girls. May I ask for a demonstration?"

Ebeny and Camilla looked at each other and grinned. "Definitely!" they replied readily.

Meanwhile, Poot and Brashong had taken a walk up to the caves up on the high wall. Looking out upon the area they now called home, they talked about Barron's secret.

«When do you think Barron will tell Ebeny and Camilla of their heritage, Poot?» Brashong asked his brother thoughtfully.

«I don't know. I do hope that he tells them soon, though. It isn't good to wait,» Poot replied. Brashong nodded at these wise words. They were enjoying the sights when, out of the corner of Brashong's left tentacle eye, he saw movement by the rock wall that hid the entrance to the valley. He stopped and turned, touching Poot's shoulder to make him stop, too. Poot's head turned and he saw what Brashong was seeing.

Now, moving slowly across the outskirts of the valley, a small horde of evil beings made their way to a niche in the wall that their leader made into a cave with a wave of his hand. Once they were all in, the leader turned around and sealed the gaping hole. In astonishment, the two brothers galloped down the rock face at full speed. They needed to warn Barron. Only one person could do that other than Barron, but Barron was in the Gathering Cavern with his daughters, Ga, Sorin, and Shamoola. They shuddered at the thought that slowly crept into their heads. It couldn't be, but the trick they had just seen performed with the rock wall confirmed their worst fear.

It was Gorgon, and he was in the valley.

"*WHAT?!*" Barron's outraged bellow echoed loudly throughout the Gathering Cavern. Poot had just finished telling Barron of his and Brashong's sighting of Gorgon, the evil sorcerer. Sorin was shaking with fear. Shamoola was nervously wringing his hands, but tried not to look too frightened. Ga buzzed around Ebeny and Camilla in worried circles.

"How could that be? You and I both made sure to magically lock the door from the inside," Shamoola said as he stood up from his seat on the cave floor.

"We obviously underestimated the power of Gorgon. It seems that he has somehow acquired the elfin touch," Barron grimly stated.

"Barron, shall I go see if I can hear anything?" Ga asked him. Camilla's face showed fear for her friend, but Barron ignored her fear and let him go out the cave entrance.

A little while later, Ga zoomed back into the cave. "I stopped by where Poot said that he and Brashong saw the hideous group disappear. My mechanical ears are highly sensitive and I overheard an important conversation." He paused long enough to get to the center of the group.

"I heard that they were planning an ambush on us while we were least expecting it. Someone said that half of their group would gather at the base of this mountain and wait until we come down. The other half would block us off if we would try to escape."

"What will we do, Barron?" Sorin asked pitifully.

"What will we do you ask?" Barron paused dramatically and raised a clenched fist high in the air. "We will meet them in battle."

Chapter 27

Fire and Ice

Ebeny, Sorin, Camilla, Ga, Poot, Brashong, Shamoola, and
Barron walked down the mountain. They were heading
to the bottom of the mountain. If none of Gorgon's army was
there, they would march to where the gallop brothers said the
small force was hiding. New swords hung in new scabbards at
the sisters' sides, and ivy-etched bows hung across their shoulders as well as a full quiver of arrows. Fortunately, Barron and
Shamoola, on a previous exploration of the valley, had found
a cave that still contained a few weapons from the time the

elves had inhabited the valley. Battle-worn, but dependable swords hung by Barron's and Shamoola's sides. Sorin clutched small spears tightly in his talons intending to throw them at the enemy. Poot and Brashong carried short swords, and Poot carried a bow and a quiver of arrows over his shoulder. Camilla made the pets stay in the gathering cave and away from the battle.

It was early morning. The sun was just beginning to pierce the dark of night. After Barron's passionate declaration the night before, some were convinced they should attack that very moment, but logic soon overshadowed their enthusiasm. Darkness would quickly fall, and reason dictated that they should wait till daybreak to meet Gorgon. During the night, they prepared what they could and tried to sleep in shifts. Sleep, however, came fitfully, when it came at all. To make sure that Gorgon's army didn't ambush them in their sleep, Ga periodically zoomed to Gorgon's cave and returned to give reports on everything that he heard.

Now, as the little band of friends traveled down the mountain, all was quiet. No one dared to make any noise. They stopped at the base of the mountain. Barron called them together.

"Okay, everyone. This is it. Gorgon will probably be here soon. I'm sure his spies have already reported that we have left the safety of our cave. When Gorgon's army comes close enough, Camilla, Ebeny, and Poot will fire arrows into their midst. Once their arrows are gone, and Gorgon's army is only a few yards away, we charge in a half-moon formation with Ebeny and Camilla in the middle. We will fight till we have no more breath left in us." Everyone nodded gravely. Barron took Camilla and Ebeny aside. "Listen to me. Do not go after

Gorgon. You can't handle his power yet. I will take care of him." Camilla and Ebeny nodded, yet the sisters knew they would face Gorgon if they had to.

Everyone walked to where they were supposed to be. Camilla stared ahead of her and felt a nervous feeling grow in her stomach. From behind, Ebeny whispered in Camilla's ear, "Please, Camilla, stay with me no matter what."

Camilla turned her head to the side and whispered back, "I will, just as long as you do the same for me." Each of the girls nodded before reaching eagerly for the other's trembling hand.

This may be the last time I get to see the only people who understand me and love me, Camilla thought, heavy-heartedly. Looking around her at the protective circle of friends, Camilla thought how lucky she and her sister were to have such loyal friends. In school, even though Ebeny and Camilla both had friends, they had always felt strangely out of place. After all that had happened, she now understood why she had felt so awkward on Earth. She knew she belonged in Zeoch.

Ga zoomed just behind the sisters at eye level. Ebeny and Camilla turned to face him. "Girls, you are two of the most talented elves I've ever known. You should be proud of yourselves, because I know I am." Camilla and Ebeny smiled.

"Thanks, Ga," Ebeny said.

"It means a lot to hear you say that," Camilla added.

Ga was about to reply when Ebeny pointed at something. Following Ebeny's shaking finger, they noticed a dark smudge at the other side of the valley. Fear clutched her stomach. Hoping she was wrong, she looked closer and saw to her dismay a sizeable amount of different creatures coming toward them. Glancing at Poot, who stood protectively beside Ebeny, and Brashong, who stood just behind Camilla, Camilla knew that they saw them, too. Twisting her head, she looked at Barron, her new-found father. He looked at her with fierce warmth glowing in his eyes and nodded. Letting go of Ebeny's hand, she reached behind her and grabbed onto her bow.

"Bows ready," Camilla announced as she slid her hand from the top of the bow onto the grip. Poot and Ebeny nodded as they, too, reached for their bows. She waited a few moments to allow the oncoming beasts to get closer.

"Arrows ready," she announced and tried to stop her hand from trembling as she reached for an arrow and nocked it. Out of the corner of her eye, she saw Ebeny and Poot doing the same. She held her bow down in front of her, waiting until Gorgon's horde was close enough.

She stood rooted to the spot as she stared at the advancing group in front of her. As she tried to recall everything Ga had taught her about bows, Camilla remembered the other becon who had accompanied Ga on the mission to save The Last Two. Dy, the other becon, had died trying to defend their old, torn-up house. Looking yet again at the advancing group of invaders, she wondered what Dy would be doing right now if he were here. She wondered if he would be as good a friend as Ga was to her or maybe even better. Shaking her head, she scolded herself. No one could be as great a friend as Ga was.

"Are they close enough yet?" Ebeny asked, preparing to draw back her string.

"No," Camilla quickly answered.

They stood as still as statues until Camilla said, "Pull back your strings." Ebeny and Poot did as instructed.

After a few more minutes, Camilla ordered, "Archers, fire!" and three arrows flew into the air, followed by screams of pain. Camilla, Poot, and Ebeny quickly nocked their arrows and shot again and again. Each time they heard successful screams and saw bodies fall to the ground, never to rise again.

"Dang it!" Camilla muttered as she swung her bow back over her shoulder.

"What's wrong?" Ebeny asked as she fired again.

"I'm out."

"Me too," Ebeny said quietly.

«As am I,» Poot said from Camilla's right.

Camilla pulled out her sword that she had named Vanquisher, her very first sword, concocted especially for her by Froghorn and adorned by Ga. At the same time, Ebeny laid the bow back across her shoulders and drew Conqueror. Camilla heard Poot draw his sword as well.

«Camilla, Ebeny,» Poot gently pulled the sisters closer to him and put his hands gently on their shoulders. The sisters looked up into his eyes, «Just so you know, none that I have ever met has been as kind, considerate, or thoughtful as you. Be proud of who you are, daughters of Barron the sorcerer and of Ariona the elf.»

Camilla's fear melted away as a smile from ear to ear covered her face. She said, "I am proud, Poot. I'm proud of me, my dad, Ebeny, and my friends."

"I can second that," Ebeny added softly with a small smile. The big gallop's eyes shone bright with pride and happiness. Poot removed his hands from Camilla's and Ebeny's shoulders and they turned back to the attacking force led by the most feared sorcerer in Zeoch, Gorgon.

Fear crept back into Camilla when she caught sight of the horrid sorcerer, Gorgon, who was just close enough for her to see him clearly. He wore a black shirt and brown pants along with a cloak as black as his shirt. Black, dusty boots stomped along the ground. Light brown, unruly hair fluttered in the wind. A gleeful, evil expression sat on the man's pale gray face. Camilla took a step back with a look of unease on her face. It wasn't how he looked, but what she saw in his eyes that scared her. Nothing—his eyes were dull, almost lifeless. If it wasn't for the color that somehow lingered in his eyes, she would have thought that he had been a ghost.

Brashong walked up to stand beside Camilla. Slowly, Brashong drew his sword, held it in front of him, and let the sun catch the blade. As the sword shone, he said, «Stay near me, Camilla, Ebeny. I will watch over you.» The elves nodded in understanding. Looking back at Gorgon, Camilla discovered that his army was almost upon them. She tightened her grip on her sword. Though Camilla wished she could use her bow to fight, she knew combat this close required a sword.

In front of her, Barron was pointing his sword at Gorgon. In a loud, clear voice he commanded, "For my daughters, charge!" Barron, Shamoola, Ga, and Sorin let out a fierce battle cry and ran at the approaching army. The sisters, Poot, and Brashong joined in the rallying call and followed Barron.

Both sides rushed forward, meeting in the middle with a loud clang. Although Barron's fighters knew that they were outnumbered by many, they fought bravely.

A new feeling bubbled inside Ebeny and Camilla, a sense of leadership. Leaping boldly in front of Brashong, Camilla took down a bambargle in one blow. Brashong stared in awe, but only for a few seconds. Whipping around, he sliced at a gallop who was about to stab Ebeny, but received a cut himself. Sorin was hovering above, hurling sharp spears at his enemies and cackled when his spears hit their targets. Ga was flashing beam after beam at creatures to and fro. Shamoola stood underneath Ga and Sorin. He finished off those who had been hit by Sorin and Ga, but had not gone down. Poot and Ebeny, Camilla and Brashong, were fighting side by side.

Ebeny yelled, "Rashu!" at a bambargle, which exploded into dust. Ebeny swayed slightly but continued fighting.

Somewhere from behind Ebeny, she heard Camilla shout over the battle noises, "Don't use any more spells yet! Save your strength!" Ebeny nodded and began hacking away at the evil beings.

Barron chased madly after Gorgon, his arch enemy, getting blocked by fearsome creatures that ended up in pieces on the ground as he slashed and sliced with his sword. As Barron got closer to his target, more and more of Gorgon's minions ended up dead before they could even utter a sound.

Gorgon smiled wickedly. Sheathing his sword, Gorgon raised his hands and shot out a blast of ice. Barron noticed the attack quickly. He dropped to the ground and rolled right under the ice. The magic was so cold that it left his hair covered in layers of frost. Gorgon cackled wildly and didn't notice Barron leaping up and shooting a ray of bright orange fire that would have killed Gorgon if it hadn't been for a warning cry from one of his minions. The evil sorcerer dropped to the ground, but the top of his head was badly burned. He leapt up and stared at Barron racing toward him.

"Gorgon! Let us end this!" Barron called out to the evil sorcerer. Gorgon laughed viciously.

"Gladly!" Gorgon lunged at Barron, sword out-stretched. Barron met his sword with a loud clang. Sparks showered the two sorcerers as their blades crashed and clanged against each other again and again.

"You stole the only woman I loved," Gorgon angrily told Barron in between blows. "I have hated you ever since. Now, this day, I will kill you!" Gorgon twisted his sword and curved under Barron's sword. Gorgon tilted his sword upward and sliced Barron's arm. Blood began seeping immediately; it soaked into Barron's light-colored sleeve.

"Argh!" Barron shouted. He fell back a few steps and looked at his scarlet arm. All he could see was bright blood, but he guessed that the wound was deep. Barron tried hard not to think about the increasing pain, for he knew that it could get him killed. He looked back to Gorgon with surprise in his eyes.

Gorgon smiled wickedly with hatred in his eyes. "I've been practicing," the evil sorcerer admitted. Gorgon lifted his sword and prepared to charge Barron.

Barron lifted his sword with much effort. He muttered a curse. Gorgon had sliced Barron's sword arm. Barron held his sword weakly in front of him just in time to block Gorgon's blow. The blow didn't hurt Barron, but it did push him farther back.

"Ha ha ha!" Gorgon laughed as he lunged at Barron and sliced his cheek. It wasn't deep, but it stung. Barron fell back even more. He lifted his hand and lightly touched the blood running down his face. He closed his eyes for a few seconds to try and block out the pain. He lifted his sword and opened his eyes. Stepping back one more step, Barron found himself up against a mountain wall.

"I have you just where I want you," Gorgon chuckled to himself.

Barron took a deep breath and moved forward a step. He lifted his sword and took a swing at Gorgon, who blocked it easily. Barron muttered a spell under his breath, and Gorgon flew backwards. Barron quickly muttered another spell, and vines from the mountainsides slowly slithered down and wrapped themselves around Gorgon's waist, arms, and legs. The evil sorcerer struggled to free himself.

Barron walked over to Gorgon and glared down at him.

"Now *I* have you just where I want you," He mocked Gorgon with a slight smile. The smile soon disappeared as Barron said to Gorgon, "You were the cause of Ariona's death, the death of so many innocent beings, of my distress and sadness over the years, and the reason my daughters have had to grow up without a mother." Barron lifted his sword and gritted his teeth against the fiery pain that shot up his arm. "You will pay for what you have done to this family."

Gorgon shook his head, hatred in his eyes. "No, Barron. I was not the cause of all this misfortune. If *you* had never taken Ariona away from me, none of this would have happened. If you hadn't existed, Ariona would be alive," Gorgon explained. Barron shook his head in disbelief.

In front of him, Gorgon muttered something Barron didn't hear, and fire licked down the vines, disintegrating them all. Gorgon rose and lifted his sword, preparing for the final strike. He whispered something else, and another vine appeared out of nowhere. It quickly wrapped itself around Barron's ankles and yanked backward. Barron fell onto his knees with a gasp of pain.

Barron looked up at the glinting blade above his head and quietly said, "Do whatever you want to me, just don't hurt my daughters."

"Oh, don't worry," Gorgon said. "I only want to have their powers. They seem very strong, and they already know some magic! Don't worry, Barron. I won't dare harm them, unless they refuse to cooperate." He added with a wicked smile.

Barron's head snapped up. He raised his sword and swung. He sliced Gorgon's leg, but the wound wasn't as deep as he had wanted.

Rising up from the ground with a new source of power, Barron growled, "Don't you dare touch those girls." He swung at Gorgon, but the evil sorcerer blocked it easily. Cackling, Gorgon raised his sword and swung at Barron's right arm again. Barron moved to block him, but just before Gorgon's sword hit Barron's, he moved it just ever so slightly. The sword's impact point was the side of Barron's stomach.

"Ahh!" Barron howled. He collapsed on the ground and began to see red. The pain was overwhelming. Gorgon laughed and walked slowly away. Barron knew he would never survive unless he used a healing spell. Although it wouldn't fix everything, it would help.

Gathering up the last of his strength, Barron muttered, "Healos," and felt a slight tingling in his stomach. Soon the pain in his stomach went away completely, and the bleeding from his other wounds stopped. He closed his eyes, but before blacking out, he thought, *Ariona, protect them.*

Back in the battle, Ebeny heard a howl of pain. She turned and saw Gorgon racing away from the limp body of her father. Ebeny gasped. "Dad," she whispered. Anger bubbled up inside of her as she yanked Camilla away with her.

"What are you doing?" Camilla asked her breathlessly.

Ebeny didn't respond. She simply pointed at Barron's bloody body and Gorgon. Camilla gasped and began to run faster.

Gorgon turned and began to walk toward the elves. The sisters mustered their courage and continued on to meet Gorgon.

"Ah, the elf sisters. You have no idea how long I have waited for this moment," Gorgon told them with a smile.

Ebeny pointed Conqueror at Gorgon and asked, "What do you mean?" Camilla glared at Gorgon and followed Ebeny's motion with her sword, Vanquisher.

"What do you mean, you ask? I knew your parents. They were both very skilled and powerful in battle. I simply assumed that you would have inherited some of that."

"So?" Camilla asked.

"So, if I had you on my side of every battle, I would practically never lose!" He laughed contentedly. "I want you to join me."

Ebeny and Camilla gaped at him. "Why would we?" Ebeny asked.

"Look what you did to our father!" Camilla added.

Gorgon shrugged. "He had it coming to him," Gorgon said, as if it were the simplest answer in the world. "But never mind him," Gorgon said. He reached out and began to lower Ebeny's and Camilla's blades. "Think about it. If you join me, you'll have power, power over everyone in Zeoch. There wouldn't be anything you couldn't do. Just imagine what you could have."

Ebeny and Camilla let their eyes drift back to Barron's bloody body. They missed him already. Turning back to each other, Ebeny and Camilla locked eyes and quickly decided their answer.

Ebeny looked back to Gorgon. "That sounds nice, Gorgon," she began. Gorgon nodded happily, a smile on his face. "But we know that you just killed our father and that you caused that battle long ago where we lost our mother. Besides, we aren't that interested in power." Gorgon's smiled melted, and he tightened his grip on his sword.

"Our answer is no," Camilla told him and raised her sword once more. Ebeny followed her lead.

"Then you have chosen to be eliminated," Gorgon growled. He slashed at Camilla, who blocked it easily.

Ebeny hollered, "Linka!" A bright light erupted from her and blinded Gorgon. At the same time Camilla shouted, "Mitle!" and Gorgon's sword clattered to the ground. Raising her sword, Ebeny slashed out at Gorgon, but he sidestepped. Instead of inflicting a fatal wound, Ebeny's sword sliced off the fingers of Gorgon's left hand. He fell to the ground.

Yowling in pain, he grappled for his sword with his uninjured hand. Finally finding his grip, he swung up, over, and around with it. With quicker reflexes than ever seen before, Camilla dodged the attempts easily and smiled. Growling with pain and fury, Gorgon twisted his sword around in a circle. Blocking it with ease, Ebeny counterattacked, with Camilla copying on her left side. Camilla's swing missed her mark, but Ebeny's found hers straight on. A puddle of blood appeared on the ground from a gash in Gorgon's side. A massive chunk was missing from his right side. Ribs were grazed and some were broken. He gasped and snarled in pain. Leaping out at them, he swung his sword, missing the girls by an inch. He swung again and caught them off guard. The flat side of the sword smacked both sisters right on the head, hard. It knocked them out cold. He brought it around again and slashed both their arms when they hit the ground. When their arms healed, they would have something to remember Gorgon by.

A loud clang echoed throughout the valley after Gorgon's sword slammed into the wall from his second swing. Upon hearing the sound, Ga turned. Seeing Camilla and Ebeny on the ground made him mad; seeing red blood appear on both of their arms made him furious. Racing over to them, he opened up his underbelly to have a short sword appear in the grasp of metal hands. Yowling, he swung the sword at Gorgon ferociously. Surprised by this, Gorgon had no time to duck. The well aimed swing hit him in the back. Provoked, he twisted around and aimed at Ga. He swerved aside easily.

"Never...touch...them...again!!!" His eyes turned red with rage. His mechanical hands thrust forth the sword that hit Gorgon in the back again, but this time piercing him all the way through. A confused frown crossed Gorgon's face. In one last attempt, he swung the sword at Ga and sliced him in half.

By this time the others in Gorgon's army had fled. Shamoola led Sorin, Poot, and Brashong over, ready to fight, but all they came upon was a sad sight. Ebeny and Camilla had almost awakened completely from the blow and were gazing sleepily at both of their scarlet arms.

Behind them, Barron blinked his eyes open. He was surprised to find that the only thing left from Gorgon's attack was the blood around him and on him, as well as three nasty scars that were hard to see through the blood. He rose and looked around. His eyes rested on his daughters, and an uneasy feeling bubbled up inside of him. He began to walk urgently over to them.

Gorgon's face had turned the color of a sheet of paper. His clothes and cloak were soaked with his own blood. He glared at the girls with pure hatred burning in his eyes and said with his last breath, "I will be back; mark my words; I will." Then with a shudder, he fell to the ground. His slumped figure shimmered and disappeared.

Barron had finally reached them and knelt down behind Ebeny and Camilla. He laid his hands on their shoulders.

Ebeny and Camilla whipped around. "Dad!" they screamed together and flung their arms around him. Barron grunted and much more slowly wrapped his arms around his daughters.

"But we thought you were dead!" Ebeny said as they finally pulled apart.

Barron smiled. "I have lots of surprises." He laughed. Ebeny and Camilla hugged him once more before pulling away. Barron, Ebeny, and Camilla sat back. Shamoola, Poot, Brashong, and Sorin went over to Barron and told him how relieved they were that he had survived the battle. Shamoola laid his hand on Barron's shoulder and smiled down at his old friend.

When they were all done, everyone turned to Ga. The becon had been completely severed in half, and not even a wire was connecting him. His lights were flickering on and off. His once full and happy eyes were now dull and sad.

Camilla crawled over to him with Ebeny not far behind. His words could hardly be heard, "Do not despair. I am only one life in a big world. Your lives will go on." Tears streamed down Camilla's distressed face.

"No, no you can't go, I need you, please," Camilla sobbed. Ebeny reached a hand over to her sister's shoulder. Camilla shook it off and bent lower, ignoring the increasing pain in her arm.

"Oh, Camilla my dear, this is how it needs to be." He paused, "But I want you to know that there is no other way I would want to die. If I could save you, it would be worth my whole life and many more." With that said, his eyes dulled to a gray, before turning off forever.

Everyone around them knelt in a silent respect for their lost friend who had died saving those he cared about most. Ga, the becon, was dead.

CHAPTER 28

A New home

"Here, here is good." Camilla directed the digging crew sadly. Sorin and Ebeny laid the bandaged Ga in a shallow hole freshly dug that morning. Shamoola covered him with sand and dirt; it was something she couldn't bear to see. Camilla helped carve Ga's name into a big stone and left as Brashong and Poot carefully laid the stone on top of a great friend.

The sisters quietly walked away from Ga's grave by the door that linked the Secret Valley of the Elves to the outside world. Camilla had tears running down her cheeks. Ebeny's eyes were misty as well. As they walked, Ebeny hugged her heavy-hearted sister. She knew that her sister still grieved greatly for their lost companion, Ga the becon. Laying her arm across her sister's shoulders, she squeezed reassuringly and headed toward their father, who was standing by the lake shore. Barron had not helped to bury Ga. When they got there, they stood quietly without talking.

"What are you doing?" Ebeny asked him as she slid her hand into his.

"Thinking," Barron replied without turning to look at his daughters.

"About what?" Camilla asked.

"Something Gorgon said to me," Barron answered.

"What did he say?" Ebeny asked.

Barron turned his head to look at her. His eyes were confused. "He didn't want her to die," he plainly said.

Camilla looked at Ebeny before saying, "Who? Our mother?"

Barron nodded and looked back to the lake. "You remind me of her a lot," he said and smiled at the sisters.

"Really?" Ebeny asked.

"Yes, more than you know."

"How do we remind you, Dad?" Camilla asked.

"Well, you and Ebeny are both determined, you have kind hearts, you are incredibly smart, and you are skilled in magic, Also, you two inherited your mother's stunning beauty." Barron explained. Ebeny and Camilla beamed with happiness.

The three of them stood in silence for a long while simply staring at the softly rippling lake. Finally, Barron spoke.

"Gorgon was truthful you know," he said to his daughters. Camilla looked up at his expressionless face questioningly. Ebeny did the same.

"When he said that he would return, he was right. I don't believe that you understood him correctly." Ebeny shook her head while Camilla gazed into the lake. She didn't want to think about Gorgon.

"How could he do that, Dad?" Ebeny asked, clearly confused by this.

"Well, Gorgon has an ability to wrap his soul around others until he can regenerate. I don't know who he did that to, but I do know that we should keep quiet until we know more about this." He turned and started to walk away.

"Oh," Barron walked back to his daughters. "The others said that I should tell you this soon, so…" He paused thoughtfully. "Your mother wanted me to tell you this when as you were old enough to understand and take it seriously." Barron knelt and pulled Ebeny and Camilla closer by their hands. "You're princesses." Ebeny and Camilla stared at their father's serious eyes for a few seconds. After a while, they realized that he was telling the truth.

"W-w-wha …how?" Ebeny stuttered. Camilla nodded. They were both clearly baffled.

"Well, I am the son of the great King Alend. I was his only child. Ariona's father was nothing more than a poor old man who had somehow raised a family. We met when I had luckily escaped my royal life—"

Ebeny cut him off. "Didn't you like being a prince?"

Barron shook his head. "I didn't like people doing everything for me and always asking me 'Do you need anything, sir?' 'Would you like another ink bottle, sir?' 'What color do you think: red or blue?' It drove me crazy. Anyway, I was walking in the forest one day, when out of nowhere stepped a beautiful young maiden. Her hair caught the sun and burned like fire with streaks of sunlight. Her eyes were just like sapphires." Camilla's and Ebeny's eyes brightened from hearing how lovely their mother was. "We fell in love the first time our eyes met.

"Our parents approved of our love and planned our wedding. We lived happily in the castle, and eventually, I became king. Ariona was queen, and we had two beautiful princesses." His face darkened before continuing his story.

"The year after you were born, Ebeny, was the year Gorgon tried to overthrow us. It was horrible; almost every single good creature and man was killed except a few who escaped. Until I came back, Shamoola, my good friend, was called king in my place."

"Whoa," Camilla remarked softly.

"Definitely," Ebeny added quietly. The sisters hugged the king and stood up. King Barron stood, nodded to his daughters, and walked off.

Ebeny and Camilla stood by the lake in silence, each in their own thoughts. Ebeny finally broke the silence. "You know, it is all right to still be sad about Ga. He was a good friend." Camilla looked at Ebeny with grief-filled eyes.

"Yeah, he was," She sighed heavily. "I miss him already." A single tear crept out of Camilla's eyes. Ebeny nodded and leaned her head on Camilla's shoulder. She was about to say something when an astonished look crossed Camilla's face. Ebeny straightened up immediately. With sudden realization, Camilla understood what her dream had meant.

"A friend shall go who is dearest to you, but one who is not expected." *So that is what that had meant,* Camilla suddenly felt as stupid as the mice that walk right into traps. It had been obvious whom the prophecy had been talking

about. *If there had only been a way to save him. I would've done anything.*

"What is it Camilla? Did you see something?" Ebeny asked, very concerned.

"Oh, no, I didn't see anything. Don't worry. Nothing's wrong." Camilla did her best to smile at her sister. Ebeny nodded, but knew that Camilla was not telling her something very important. She dismissed the matter and gazed at the valley around her.

Looking over at Camilla, she said, "This is it, Camilla, the Secret Valley of the Elves."

Camilla stared at her. "What are you talking about?"

Ebeny sighed. For a deep thinker, Camilla sure didn't pick up on things quickly.

"Just think about it, Camilla. Our old home is wrecked and probably burned to the ground by now. We need a new one, but we can't go back to Earth." Camilla's face brightened as she understood what her sister was trying to tell her.

"Yes, this is our home. I can feel it. Although it isn't perfect, we can make it work." Grabbing hands, they raced to their cavern, laughing the whole way. They sat in the entrance until Camilla could see stars that were shining brighter than she had thought possible; the moon was like a beacon in a lighthouse. Ebeny and Camilla said goodnight to each other and gathered their pets. Ebeny and Sparkle huddled together on the cool cave floor. Ingline nestled closer to Squeaker, who nestled closer to Camilla who had curled into a ball.

She's right, Camilla thought happily, *this is our one and only home. One day, we will defeat Gorgon once and for all, and I will avenge Ga's death, but until then, we will wait for the perfect time.*

A Note From the Author

When I started this book, I was only 9 years old. When I finished it, I was 11. I have wanted to be an author and have people enjoy my writing since I was in first grade. I am now 12 as I watch my book being published, which is a dream come true for me. The message that I want you, the reader, to take away from this book and my achievements is that if you have a dream, don't ever stop trying to accomplish it.

About Kaden Hurley

Kaden Hurley, age 12, lives in Pennsylvania with her mother, father, sister, and collie-lab mix named Siya. Writing is Kaden's passion, but when she's not writing, she's reading fantasy novels, playing her clarinet, playing softball, cheerleading for the Big Spring Bulldogs, or spending time with her family and friends. *Elves of Zeoch: The Last Two* is her first novel.